THANK YOU, JACKIE ROBINSON

"The St. George Hotel?" I interrupted. "Is that anywhere near Ebbets Field?"

"Not far," Davy answered. "You ever been to Ebbets Field?"

"No," I replied. "I've never been."

"It's a nice ball park," he commented. "Small, but nice."

Inside of myself I was so excited that I felt like I was standing on my head. I knew something big was going to happen. But I didn't let my excitement show. I just said, really cool, "You like the Dodgers?"

Davy smiled. "Like the Dodgers? The Dodgers with me is like egg salad with you. There just isn't any other ball team. How about you? What ball team do you like?"

"Me?" I answered. "Oh, I feel the same. There isn't any other ball team."

THANK YOU, JACKIE ROBINSON

by Barbara Cohen

DRAWINGS BY
Richard Cuffari

A Beech Tree Paperback Book   New York

Text copyright © 1974 by Barbara Cohen
Illustrations copyright © 1974 by Richard Guffari

The Library of Congress has cataloged the Lothrop, Lee & Shepard Books edition of *Thank You, Jackie Robinson* as follows: Cohen, Barbara. Thank you, Jackie Robinson. Summary: A fatherless white boy, who shares with an old black man an enthusiasm for the Brooklyn Dodgers and first baseman Jackie Robinson, takes a ball autographed by Jackie to his elderly friend's death bed. ISBN 0-688-07909-1 [1. Brooklyn Dodgers (Baseball team)— Fiction. 2. Robinson, Jackie, 1919–1972—fiction. 3. Baseball—Fiction. 4. Friendship— Fiction] I. Guffari, Richard, 1925–1978, ill. II. Title. PZ7. C6595Th 1988 [Fic] 87-29341

First Beech Tree Edition, 1997
ISBN 0-688-15293-7
12 13 LP/BR 20 19

FOR LOUIS

Listen. When I was a kid, I was crazy. Nuttier than a fruitcake. Madder than a hatter. Out of my head. You see, I had this obsession. This hang-up. It was all that mattered to me.

I was in love with the Brooklyn Dodgers.

"So what's so funny about that?" you might say. "So I'm in love with the Boston Celtics." Or the Miami Dolphins. Or the Los Angeles Rams. Or the New York Rangers. Or the Chicago Black Hawks.

Take it from me, whatever it is you're in love with— it's not the same thing. Suppose on May 18, 1947, you had asked me, "Who did the Dodgers play on August 4, 1945?" I would have answered, "The Braves."

But that's not all. I could go on. "They lost a double-header in Boston. But it wasn't a real double-header.

The first game took only twelve minutes—it was the end of a game which had been suspended June 17 on account of the Sunday curfew and the Braves won 4-1.

"The Braves won the regular contest too, 1-0. Bill Lee pitched for the Braves, Vic Lombardi for the Dodgers. Maybe Lombardi did lose but he pitched a terrific game. It was that dumb umpire's fault he lost, anyway. What was his name, that dumb umpire? Oh, yeah—George Magerkurth—dumb George Magerkurth. Lombardi walked Dick Culler in the first. Phil Masi came up next. Culler was suddenly trapped far off base, and the Braves' coach called, 'Balk.' Real fast, Lombardi threw the ball to Augie Galan at first base who threw it to Eddie Stanky at second. Magerkurth pointed to second base. Stanky and all the others thought this meant that he was calling a balk. Culler trotted to second, Stanky didn't tag him, and then the dumb umpire said he hadn't called a balk! Stanky and Leo Durocher really blew their stacks, but Magerkurth didn't throw them out of the ball game. He must have felt guilty about what he'd done. That proves he made a mistake, don't you think . . . ? Culler advanced to third on Masi's long fly to Dixie Walker and scored on Ducky Medwick's long hit, also to Dixie. That was the ball game, right there in the first inning, though no one knew it then. . . ."

If you didn't stop me, I'd go on. I'd give you the whole game in just that way—like a playback of Red Barber's broadcast over WHN. But it wasn't a playback. I wasn't secretly memorizing tapes up in my bedroom. There weren't any tapes. There weren't any tape recorders. All I had was every record book money could buy and a portable radio my rich aunt had given me for my birthday. Battery-operated, it was a great big thing that I used to lug with me everywhere during the season. Except to school. They wouldn't let me bring it to school. After all, it wasn't like I could hide it, the way kids can hide transistors today. You kids, you know how lucky you are? I used to have to miss the World Series. I had to read about it in the paper. Can you imagine that? I hope they feel sorry now, those teachers, for the way they messed me up.

Anyway, I could give you the whole game, play by play, for any day during the whole period I had been hooked on the Brooklyn Dodgers. Just like that. Without looking at any books or papers or anything. I remembered it, like you might remember Christmas day, 1973, when they gave you your own portable color TV. Or March 3, 1971, the day you finally beat up the big kid who'd stolen your pack of twelve different-colored magic markers.

I didn't remember those games because I had some kind of super memory or something. I couldn't remember if the Japanese had surrendered to the Americans on August 4, 1945. I couldn't remember if my grandmother had come to visit us that day. I couldn't remember if I'd had my favorite meal for supper. I couldn't remember anything that had actually happened to me. I could only remember those games.

That's not normal. That's sick. But that's how it was.

I didn't seem sick. I mean, I got promoted each June and played baseball in the schoolyard with the other guys. Of course, I was this real scrungy kid, about half the size of all the others, so I got picked last for the teams, but there was no malice in that and I didn't really mind. Not too much.

Only one guy ever really knew just how nuts I was. Since no one else really knew how much I loved the Brooklyn Dodgers, no one ever thought I was sick. No one ever took me to a psychiatrist or anything like that. Not even to a regular doctor. Except once, in 1951, when the Dodgers got in a play-off with the Giants for the pennant, and I developed this tic. My left eye kept twitching all the time. My mother took me to the doctor then and he asked what was I nervous about. My mother, who was a pretty shrewd number even though I didn't tell her much, said, "The National League pennant race," so the doctor gave me some belladonna and said to come back if I still had the twitch after the World Series. I didn't, so I never had to go back.

Eventually, I grew out of it of course. I mean, I'm much older now. I go about my business just like anybody else. I'm not locked up in some nut house or anything like that, so I must have grown out of it. I grew out of it before anybody really noticed just about how crazy I was. Except this one guy, like I said. But, see, he didn't think I was crazy. He thought being in love with the Brooklyn Dodgers was just the way you were supposed to be. Of course, he couldn't recite every play of every game for every season that he'd been following the Brooklyn Dodgers. But he didn't think there was anything funny about my being able to do it. He just thought it was a kind of talent I had, like being able to play "God Bless America" on a comb wrapped in toilet paper the way my buddy Mickey did. Maybe that's what it was—a talent. Or maybe all kids are crazy. And maybe Davy—he's the guy I'm talking about—maybe Davy knew that.

Davy was my best friend. He was this great big black guy, about sixty years old. Only in those days we didn't say "black guy." Nobody said that. We were very careful to say "Negro," or maybe "colored." Never "nigger." Saying "nigger" if you were a middle-class Jewish boy whose folks had voted for Roosevelt four times was like using a really filthy swear word. Maybe you did it when you were with the guys, to sound big, but you never did it in front of anybody else. And, nobody ever thought of saying "black." I don't know why. We'd just never heard of it. It never even came up.

So, you might well ask, how did a scrungy, freckled-faced little Jewish kid of ten get to have for his best friend this great big black guy of sixty? That's a fair question, and I will try to answer it.

My father was dead. He had died when I was about seven. I had these three sisters. Three sisters and a mother. Wherever I turned, there was another female. Even the dog was female. She was this little tiny silver poodle. That's no kind of dog for a boy.

My mother was O.K., but I didn't get to see very much of her. She had this little inn outside of the town of Winter Hill, New Jersey. We lived in it. I guess that was O.K. too, because if we hadn't lived in it, we would never have seen her at all. But it made for a kind of odd life. We had to walk two miles to school. We didn't have any neighbors. The inn was on this busy highway. You took your life in your hands every time you crossed it. I still can't believe the four of us managed to survive crossing that highway twice every day for thirteen years. The result was we didn't have many kids for friends. It didn't bother my two little sisters, Fran and Rosy. They were only a year apart and had each other to play with. It didn't bother my older sister, Sara, very much either. She always had her nose in a book anyway. She'd stop in the library on her way home from school and she'd be set up for a week. She had a special deal going with the librarian. She was the only twelve-year-old who was allowed to take out ten books at a time. She used to have a problem lugging them the two miles home. Sometimes I helped her if I didn't see any of the other guys out on the street. Of course, I made her promise to beat up my cocoa real good the next morning so it wouldn't have any skin on it. Sara made breakfast for us. My mother went to bed too late to get up for breakfast.

Rosy and Fran had each other and Sara had her books. What did I have? The Brooklyn Dodgers, of course. But that wasn't enough. See, I wanted to tell someone about them. I wanted to do more than just replay all those games in my head. With my friends at school—well, sometimes at lunch a question would come up. "Who hit the most triples in major-league history?" Everybody knew that Babe Ruth had hit the most home runs. But had he hit the most triples? Naturally, I wouldn't say anything, because I knew, and they all knew I knew, and if I blurted the name right out, that'd spoil the fun.

But finally, some one would say, "O.K., Sammy, you

can tell us now." Then I'd say, "Chief Wilson in 1912 when he hit thirty-six triples playing for Pittsburgh." See, I knew all that kind of stuff too. I knew everything in the record book. But my friends never wanted to hear a whole game. Oh, maybe once in a while, a new kid would show up in school and they'd get a dime off of him by betting he couldn't pick a day in the last three years for which I couldn't name the entire line-up of the Brooklyn Dodgers and their opponents. But that was all. They got bored once I went into the play by play.

They all liked baseball and everything. But they'd rather play it than talk about it. They'd even rather shoot marbles than talk about it. Besides, some of them were Yankee fans, some of them were Giant fans. There were only two—Mickey and Al—who were Dodger fans, and the only reason they were Dodger fans was because you had to be a fan of some team. They didn't really care, if you know what I mean. They were both very good athletes. From September till it got cold they played football. Then they played basketball in the gym or at the Y until spring. Then they played baseball all spring and summer, every afternoon, every evening until it got dark. Sometimes I played with them. But not too often. Mom didn't go for us crossing that highway once the sun set.

One late spring day when I got home from school,

14

I went right to the kitchen for something to eat, the way I usually did. Only today I wasn't in too much of a hurry, because the Dodgers weren't scheduled. They were going to play a night game in St. Louis and the pre-game show didn't even go on the air until nine o'clock at night. If the Dodgers were playing an afternoon game, I grabbed a glass of milk and a roll and butter real fast so I could rush upstairs and catch the last couple of innings. But if they weren't playing, I could look around the kitchen and see if there was anything good left over from lunch. Something that I liked. I didn't like too many different things.

On this particular day, someone was rolling out pie dough at the long wooden work table. There was a pile of apples in a box next to the table. An apple was what I wanted. But I had never seen the man behind the table before. It was tough for me to say anything to someone I didn't know pretty well. So I stood by the swinging doors, watching him. Finally, he looked up and saw me.

"Hullo, kid," he called. "Want some apple?"

"Yes," I said. I walked over to the table.

He pushed one of the pies he was making toward me. It was all ready for the oven except that it didn't have a top crust. It was filled to overflowing with a heap of sliced apples which he had sprinkled with a

15

bunch of sugar, cinnamon, nutmeg, and globs of butter. "Take a few," he said. "No one'll miss 'em."

My mother had always bought the pies she served in the inn's restaurant at the bakery. I had never tasted sliced apples soaked in sugar and spices before. They were better than plain old apples any day of the week.

"Thanks," I said, my mouth stuffed with the fruit.

"Don't thank me," he said. "Thank Mrs. Greene. They're her apples. I hope she don't mind."

"She won't mind," I said. "I'm her son, Sam."

"I'm glad to meet you, Sam," he said. "My name's Davy." He wiped his enormous black hand on his stiff white cotton apron to get the flour off and held it out to me. I shook it.

"Are you the new cook?" I asked. I didn't pay very

much attention to arrivals and departures among the inn's employees. If they lasted six months, I spoke to them. I didn't like new people. Of course, there were some, like Guy the bartender and the waitress Annie, who had been around for so many years they were like members of my own family. But there was no point in even thinking about the ones who came and went, until it looked like they were going to stay a while. In the past few months there'd been one cook after another, and even I knew my mother was worried. One thing you have to have in even the smallest restaurant is a good cook. My mother was a good cook. But she couldn't be in the kitchen and out front running things too. So when Gustav, who'd been with her ever since my father had died, decided to go back to Sweden, she was very upset. Not me. I didn't like Gustav. He was mean. You'd never catch him feeding me apples coated with cinnamon and sugar. He didn't make pies anyway. "I am not a pastry chef," he'd say, making his long, skinny face seem even longer and skinnier. Our restaurant was too small to need two cooks. It got along with one and a salad man. That's why Mom had been buying her desserts from the bakery.

Anyway, after Gustav left, there'd been just one cook after another. They all disappeared after a week or two. The best I'd gotten from any of them when I came into the kitchen for something to eat was a cold stare and the worst was, "I don't want any rotten kids in my kitchen." Maybe that's why some of them left. Maybe they weren't used to four kids running around an inn.

But this one was different. This one invited me to eat his apples, and introduced himself. "Yes," he said, "I'm the new cook."

"I hope you stay," I said.

He seemed a little startled at my remark. Actually, I was a little startled by it too. He was the first new person I'd met in about four years I didn't feel like hiding from. "Well, I hope so too," he answered at last. "Your Mama seems like a real nice lady."

"She's O.K.," I said.

"And Fran and little Rosy—they're cute as buttons," he went on.

"You watch out for them," I warned. "They'd just as soon trip you and see you flat out on the floor as live."

"You don't say," he commented mildly. "And to look at them you'd think butter wouldn't melt in their mouths. Appearances are deceiving."

I nodded my agreement. "There's another one," I said. "She's older than me—Sara. She isn't home yet. She's at the library. She won't cause you much trouble. She's always reading. But maybe you could give her a few lessons."

"What kind of lessons?"

"Cooking lessons, naturally. She makes our breakfast. The sunnyside-up eggs are always hard and the cocoa always has skin on it."

"I'll see what I can do," Davy agreed. "And on Saturdays and Sundays, if you can wait until I come in, I'll make you pancakes for breakfast."

"I'll wait," I promised.

He sprinkled some flour on the wooden table top. Then he took a bunch of dough out of the metal bowl he'd mixed it in and began rolling it out with strong, smooth thrusts of his arms. In two seconds flat he had rolled out a top crust, put it on a pie, trimmed its edges and started on another one. And all the time he kept talking to me. "What d'you like for supper?" he asked.

"Spaghetti," I replied. "I like spaghetti best. And fried chicken."

"What else?"

"Nothing else. That's all I like."

"What about lunch? What kind of sandwiches do you want me to pack?"

"Egg salad," I said.

"What else?"

"Only egg salad. I only like egg salad."

"I guess I won't have any trouble remembering what to feed you. Don't you think you might want to try something else once in a while? How about a piece of turkey?"

I shuddered. "I hate turkey," I said. "Whenever there's a wedding dinner or something else in the banquet room, I've got to stand here and put gravy on turkey dinners. The cook puts on the stuffing and the sliced turkey. Pedro, or whoever the salad man is, he puts on the potatoes. Sara puts on the peas, I put on the gravy, and Fran and Rosy put on the parsley and cranberry sauce."

"I think that's nice," Davy said. "I've never worked in a place where the whole family pitched right in and helped."

"Where did you work before you came here?" I asked.

"The St. George Hotel, in Brooklyn." He said it very calmly, just like that—"The St. George Hotel, in Brooklyn." He went on to tell me he'd quit his job and come out here to live with his daughter, but I hardly even heard him.

"The St. George Hotel?" I interrupted. "Is that any-where near Ebbets Field?"

"Not far," Davy answered. "You ever been to Ebbets Field?"

"No," I replied. "I've never been."

"It's a nice ball park," he commented. "Small, but nice."

Inside of myself I was so excited that I felt like I was standing on my head. I knew something big was going to happen. But I didn't let my excitement show. I just said, really cool, "You like the Dodgers?"

Davy smiled. "Like the Dodgers? The Dodgers with me is like egg salad with you. There just isn't any other ball team. How about you? What ball team do you like?"

"Me?" I answered. "Oh, I feel the same. There isn't any other ball team."

"Imagine that," Davy exclaimed. "All the way out here in New Jersey, and you feel like that about the Dodgers."

"There is no major-league ball team in New Jersey," I said. "I had to pick somebody."

"What about the Yankees or the Giants?" Davy asked. "How come you didn't pick one of them?"

That was not a question to which I had ever given any thought. Actually, I couldn't remember picking the Dodgers. It seemed, instead, as if they had picked me. They had visited themselves upon me, the way God visited himself upon the prophets in the Bible. It was a mysterious thing.

Since I couldn't answer Davy's question, I asked him one of my own. "Why did *you* pick the Dodgers? Just because you were working in Brooklyn?"

"No," Davy answered thoughtfully. "I loved the Dodgers long before I went to live in Brooklyn. I loved them back before the war when they just about never won a ball game. And this year I love them better than ever. I always knew, way deep down, that they'd come through for an old colored man like me."

"You mean Jackie Robinson?" I asked.

"That's right," Davy said. "Jackie Robinson. When Branch Rickey brought Jackie up from Montreal this year, I knew I'd been a Dodger fan all this time for a reason. It's just funny the way things work out."

"Yeah," I said. "It is. I mean, it was great that you didn't have to switch teams, or anything like that."

Davy stopped rolling his piecrust for a minute and looked at me. "You're a smart kid," he said.

"What are you talking about?" I asked. I had no idea what he meant.

He shook his head. "Never mind," he said. "Have some more apples."

I shoved some of them in my mouth. We didn't say anything for a minute, but then I started to talk again.

"I *am* smart, you know," I said. "I can do something nobody else I know can do. Of course," I added honestly, "nobody really cares that I can do it. But you might, seeing how you feel about the Dodgers."

"What's that?" asked Davy. He sounded really interested.

"Name a date in the last three years. Any date."

"O.K." He didn't know what I was driving at, but he was perfectly willing to oblige me. "My birthday.

January 23. And you need a year? Let's see—1945."

"No, no," I said impatiently. "A date during the baseball season."

"Why didn't you say so in the first place? O.K. My daughter Henrietta's birthday. July 3, 1945."

"On July 3, 1945," I began, "the Brooklyn Dodgers played the Cincinnati Reds. It was not a good night for the Dodgers. They made so many mistakes the Winter Hill high school team could have beaten them. Clyde King started for the Dodgers, Frank Dasso for Cincinnati. For the Dodgers, Eddie Stanky was at second base, Goody Rosen at center field, Augie Galan left, and Dixie Walker at right. Luis Olmo played third base, Stretch Schultz first base and Eddie Basinski shortstop. Catcher Johnny Peacock and King completed the line-up. The Reds led off with Dain Clay, the center fielder, and followed him with Eric Tipton, in left field, Al Libke in right field and their first baseman, Frank McCormick, in the clean-up position. Next were Steve Mesner, third base; Kermit Wahl, shortstop; Woody Williams, second base; catcher Al Unser and finally Dasso." I stopped for a minute to chew on another piece of apple.

"Hey, that's pretty sharp," Davy exclaimed. "You can do the line-up for any game the Dodgers played in the last four years? I never heard anything like that!"

"That's nothing," I said. "I'm not finished." I went

on. "The game was in Brooklyn. Nothing much happened in the first inning. Clay, Tipton, and Libke went down, one, two, three, and so did Stanky, Rosen, and Galan. The second inning was when everything started to go wrong. Frank McCormick beat out a perfect bunt along the third-base line, and then made it to second on Steve Mesner's sacrifice. Kermit Wahl should have grounded out, but Luis Olmo kicked the ball back into the infield and McCormick made it to third. Then King picked Wahl off at first base, but Schultz's throw to Eddie Basinski hit Wahl in the back, so Wahl was safe at second and McCormick scored!

"All this may have thrown King off, because he walked Williams. Then Unser singled. Goody Rosen caught Dasso's long fly ball, but it scored Wahl and sent Williams to third. Williams and Unser both scored on singles by Clay and Eric Tipton. King allowed no more hits for the remaining three innings he worked, but it was too late. . . ."

Well, I went on like that for the whole game. And Davy listened to me tell the whole game too. He didn't say anything. Every once in a while he just shook his head in amazement, and let me continue right to the end when King was credited with his first loss of the season and Dasso with his fourth victory. The Reds won, 5-1. The Dodgers had made four errors, the Reds none. It was a disaster.

When I had finished Davy shook his head again.

"That's right," he said. "That's the way it was."

"How do you know?" I asked.

"I was there."

"You were there?" I was amazed. It was hard for me to realize that ball games were something people actually went to. I had heard them over the radio, in Red Barber and Connie Desmond's voices, but except for an occasional picture in *The New York Times* and in my baseball magazines, I saw them only in my head.

The next fall we got a T.V. set in the bar, but the spring I met Davy I had only seen one game on T.V. That was a World Series game at my friend Mickey's house. Mickey was rich.

"Yeah," Davy went on. "I was at that game, all right. Of course, I don't remember it the way you do, but I remember it was a disaster. I remember the score. I felt terrible. I always take Henrietta and her husband to a ball game for Henrietta's birthday. Most times lately my Dodgers have come through for me, but that night they sure didn't!"

Davy was the first person who had ever listened to me recite a ball game right through to the end. I felt wonderful, as if at last there was a reason for my crazy gift. But my mind was on another subject now, nothing to do with the game itself, actually. "Listen," I asked. "Did you take Henrietta's children? Do you take children to ball games too?"

"Henrietta's got no children," Davy said. "It's just one of those things. Henrietta's got no children, and I got no children except Henrietta."

After that, every day when I came home from school I talked with Davy. I followed him around the kitchen while he did his work, talking to him. Luckily, things are pretty quiet in a restaurant between three and five in the afternoon. Mostly, it's just getting ready for supper or any parties that are going on that night. Usually around four o'clock, Davy would sit down for fifteen minutes, smoke a cigarette and drink a big glass of iced coffee with lots of cream in it. Then he'd look at the sports pages of *The Daily News* and summarize the articles for me, and show me the pictures. *The Daily News* had lots more pictures of the Dodger games than *The New York Times* did. I always felt that *The New York Times* favored the Yankees. It didn't have many pictures in it anyway.

That's what we'd do if there was no game on. If there was a game on, I'd bring my portable radio down into the kitchen and we'd listen to it. As the game went along, we'd talk about each play. We missed Durocher as a manager. The Commissioner had suspended him during spring training that year on a whole lot of trumped-up charges. Between us, we sure thought we could manage better than Burt Shotton.

The inn was busy at night. I couldn't bring the radio

downstairs into the kitchen for night games. But if a night game was really crucial, or if something really important happened, like Jackie Robinson stealing second for the seventh time that season, I'd run down and tell Davy what was going on, and then rush back to my room to find out what had happened while I was gone. I got a lot of exercise that way. I also got very good at avoiding my mother on those little downstairs forays. I was always afraid she would enlist me for another gravy-serving stint. Gravy was bad enough during the winter, but during baseball season I just didn't have time for it.

Every once in a while, Davy would make me tell him a game. He'd especially do this on days when there was no game on the radio. "Boy," he said to me once, "I used to think all those winter days without ball games were the most boring days in the world. Nothing to look forward to all winter long. But now I know you, and I can have any game I want, any time I want it. Next to Jackie Robinson, Sam, you're the best thing that ever happened to me!"

To tell you the truth, it got so I hated Davy's day off.

One afternoon, just a month or so after Davy had come to work at the inn, I met Henrietta. She came to the inn to pick Davy up to take him to the doctor. Except that she was a lady, and younger, and had lots of hair, I thought she looked just like him. She was nearly as big as he was, and just as black, and she had the same wide, warm smile. Your immediate friendship was what she expected, and no one, not even me, could bear to disappoint her.

"If I didn't drag him, old Pops here would never go to the doctor," she said to me after Davy had introduced us. "He'd just keep on complaining of those pains in his chest and never get to the doctor at all."

"I'm going, ain't I?" Davy said, a little annoyed. "What you bothering the boy with your chatter for?"

"That's O.K.," I said. "I'm not bothered."

"Hey listen, Henrietta," Davy said. "We got a minute? I want the boy here to show you something."

"Now, hold on, Pop," Henrietta said. "Don't think you can worm out of it this time. . . ."

"I promised I'd go, and I'll go," Davy said. "This'll just take a minute. Now listen, Henrietta. You tell Sam a date—any date at all during the last four baseball seasons."

"O.K.," Henrietta said. "I think you're both crazy, but O.K. April 27, 1946."

"There was no game that day," I said. "It was called on account of bad weather. Not just rain, but sleet and all that."

She looked at me kind of funny, and she said, "Well, then, April 28, 1946."

"This one is easy," I said, "because it's only last year. I can still remember what that game sounded like. So early in the season, and the Dodgers had already beaten the Giants four times. But unfortunately on April 28, 1946, the Giants took a double-header from the Dodgers, 7-3 and 10-4, breaking a Dodger winning streak of eight games. Luckily, the Cubs took both games of a double-header from St. Louis that day, too, so the Dodgers remained in first place. It wasn't as bad as it sounded, first off. The worst of it, really, was that Goody Rosen, who had been traded to the Giants only a day or two before, hit three singles! He was mad at being traded, I guess, and really got his revenge.

"It started out bad, right from the beginning. Jesse Pike hit a three-run homer in the first inning, sending starting pitcher Joe Hatten back to the dugout. He was replaced by . . ."

Henrietta listened to me in rapt fascination until I got to the fifth inning of the first game. Then she looked at her watch and interrupted me.

"Heavens, Sam, that's really something," she said. "I never heard anything like it! I thought Pop and me were Dodger fans, but you're too much! Much too much!"

"He can do that for any day," Davy said proudly.

"Humph! That sure does beat all," Henrietta said. "I'd really like to hear the end of that game, but I got to get old Pops to the doctor."

"Oh, anytime," I said airily. "My pleasure."

Henrietta's eyes opened real wide, like she had an idea, and she turned to Davy. "Listen, Pops, next time we go to a ball game, you bring Sam here along. Seeing that he's got no daddy and his mama so busy all the time, I bet he don't get much chance to go to ball games."

"I've never been to one in my whole life!" I said.

"See?" Henrietta said. "What'd I tell you?"

"I've thought of it," Davy said. "But Henrietta, do you think it'd be all right?" There was a doubtful note in his voice I'd never heard before.

"Of course, it'd be all right," I shouted. "It'd be wonderful."

"Look here, boy," Davy said sharply. "I wasn't talking to you. I was talking to Henrietta."

Davy was rarely cross with me, and his tone of voice cut me right down. But still, the idea of going to a ball game was so thrilling to me that I could not shut up entirely. "I'm sure it'd be all right with my mother," I said quietly. "I'm sure it would be."

"We'll ask her," Davy said. "And then we'll see."

Well, that's how I got to see my first major-league ball game.

The very next day, when my mother came into the kitchen, Davy said to her, "Mrs. Greene, there's something I've been meaning to ask you."

"What is it, Davy?" Mother said. She really liked Davy. He had his faults. He spent a lot of time drinking iced coffee with cream. But unlike many chefs, he had a calm, easy-going disposition. No matter how busy the inn got, he was never rattled. Besides, he was a wonderful cook. People were starting to come to the inn just to eat Davy's pies.

"I've been thinking about it for a while now," Davy answered. "Henrietta brought it to my attention yesterday that I've been wrong in not bringing it up before this." I couldn't understand why Davy was hesitating. Usually, he just came out and said whatever he wanted to say. Or at least, he did with me. With my mother, maybe, he was different.

"You know how Sam loves baseball . . ." Davy went on.

"Yes, I know," Mother said.

"It's very important for a boy," Davy continued.

"I agree," Mother said.

"It's very important for a boy to be with men and do men things."

"I couldn't agree more," Mother said. "I regret that circumstances . . ."

"Well, with you for a mother, Sam's better off than lots of kids who've got two parents," Davy said.

"Thank you, Davy," Mother said. She didn't say anything else, and neither did Davy. Finally she added, "Is that what you wanted to say to me?"

"Oh—no," said Davy. "I wanted to ask if I could take Sam to the ball game with me next time I go."

Mother hesitated for a moment.

"Please let me go," I said. "Please let me go. I'll put gravy on the turkey from now till doomsday if you'll let me go."

"Henrietta and her husband Elliot will be going too," Davy said. "You know my son-in-law Elliot Barnes, don't you? He's worked for Mr. Steinhauer down at the Oldsmobile agency for years. Born and bred right here in Winter Hill."

My mother spoke very quickly then. "Of course I know Elliot," she said. "I know he's a very fine man. But whether he goes or not doesn't matter. I'd be happy for Sam to go to the ball game with you, no matter who else goes. I was only hesitating because of school."

"Oh, don't worry about that," Davy hurried to say. "Don't worry about that. We were planning to go after vacation begins. Not until school's out."

"Well, if that's the case, I couldn't possibly object, could I?" Mother said with a smile. "If he's no trouble to you," she added.

"No trouble, Mrs. Greene," Davy said. "I invited him, didn't I?"

At first I thought I'd take my whole big loose-leaf

notebook with me to the ball game. In that notebook I had the box score of every Dodger game for the previous four years, plus various other notations about anything at all unusual that had gone on in the games. But then I decided I'd look kind of dumb carrying that notebook into the ball park, like I was going to school. I just put my assignment pad and pencil in my pocket so I could make a box score as I watched the game and transfer it to my notebook when I got home. I didn't even know that on the program they gave you a box-score form all printed up.

Sara gave me an orange and some Rice Krispies and milk for breakfast. It was summer and in the summer, thank God, Sara did not make cocoa with skin on it. I was too excited to eat much anyway.

Mother came in while the four of us were still eating breakfast at the table in the big dining room that was nearest the swinging kitchen doors. It was early for her to be awake, let alone fully dressed. But she was.

"Sam," she said, "I came down to make you some egg-salad sandwiches to take along."

"Thanks, Mom, but I don't need them," I replied. "Davy says we'll eat hot dogs at the ball park."

Mother nodded. "O.K.," she said, "but you pay for your own hot dogs. I'll get you the money." I followed her into the office. She opened up the safe and gave me a dollar. Then she gave me another one. "If you can," she said, "you treat Henrietta and Elliot and Davy to a hot dog and soda too."

"O.K.," I said. I put the money carefully in my wallet. Then Fran and Rosy burst into the office to say that Davy had come. He was waiting for me in the kitchen.

I raced out of the office. "Goodbye," Mother called after me. "Have fun."

"Goodbye, goodbye," shouted Fran and Rosy.

I threw my hand out in a hasty wave. In another minute Davy and I were seated in the back of Elliot's black Oldsmobile. Elliot and Henrietta were in the front.

"Sure beats riding in my old Chevy, don't it?" Davy asked.

"I don't know," I answered. "I've never ridden in your old Chevy."

"One of these days you'll have to." Davy said. "Elliot can't always get a weekday off."

It would happen again. This first time was not to be the last time.

It would not have been surprising if I had been disappointed in that double-header. Lots of times a person looks forward to something so anxiously that when it actually happens, it's a letdown. I had imagined so many games, picturing them in my mind, that it was always possible an actual game might be so different from what I'd imagined that I'd feel cheated. Like when you read a book, and see the movie of it afterwards, tho movie never looks the way you thought it would.

But I was not disappointed. It was even better than I had imagined, and certainly a lot better than it had looked on that tiny television screen in Mickey's house. I had not known it would be so bright, or so full of color.

We bought general-admission seats and sat high up in the bleachers, but Davy knew Ebbets Field well and he made sure that we got seats in the shade. We arrived an hour and a half before the first game of the double-header was supposed to start, so there was no problem in getting just the seats we wanted. Davy liked to get there real early so he could watch batting practice. When I looked around the empty stands, I knew I was lucky to have come with Davy. Not many people bothered to show up for batting practice.

Far below me, the grass was greener than any grass I had ever seen. I wondered how they got it so green here in Brooklyn, when it was never so green out in New Jersey where I lived. The white and gray of the ball players' uniforms showed up brilliantly against the grass. Though the players seemed quite small because they were so far away, I could read the numbers on the backs of their uniforms without any difficulty. So that really was Dixie Walker, that really was Pee

Wee Reese, and that really was Ralph Branca, in the flesh. And that one, over there, loping slowly onto the field, that really was Jackie Robinson himself.

Elliot tapped me on the shoulder. I jumped. I had been so enraptured with what was going on on the field that I had not even heard him speak to me. "Hey, Sammy," he said, "would you like to make a little wager on this game?"

Elliot was a very nice man. I mean, I liked Elliot and everything, so it really hurts me to say this about him, but he was not a Dodger fan. He was a Giant fan. The New York Giants. The New York baseball Giants. And on this day the Dodgers were in first place, the Giants five games behind in third. Elliot wanted the Dodgers to lose.

"What d'ya say?" Elliot reiterated. "A small bet— let's say twenty-five cents, even money."

"You want me to bet on the Dodgers?" I asked, puzzled.

"Well, I certainly don't want to bet on them," Elliot said. "I'll take the Cubs and you take the Dodgers. Even money."

"No," I said. "I won't do that. I won't bet on the Dodgers."

"Why not? Don't you think they're going to win?"

"Of course they're going to win," I replied. "They're certainly going to beat the crap out of a sixth-place team like Chicago."

"Well, then," Elliot insisted, "you ought to be willing to put your money where your mouth is. If a quarter's too much, we'll make it a dime. Or even a nickel."

"Not even a penny," I said firmly. "Not one red cent."

"Why not?" Elliot repeated. "Why not? I never heard there was nothing in the Jewish religion against gambling."

"Leave the boy alone," Henrietta said sharply. "If he don't want to bet, he's got more sense than you."

Well, I felt bad. Now Henrietta was mad at Elliot, and he certainly had meant no harm. He was just being friendly. "I don't have anything against gambling," I said. "I always put fifty cents in the Mother's Day pool." At the inn, there was always a pool on holidays. Everyone tried to guess how many customers we'd serve that day.

"It isn't any different, betting on a ball game," Elliot said.

By this time we were all standing up for "The Star-Spangled Banner." "I'd jinx them," I whispered quickly, and then picked up the song at the top of my lungs:

> The rocket's red glare
> The bombs bursting in air
> Gave proof through the night
> That our flag was still there . . .

But when the national anthem was over and the game had begun, Elliot still would not let the matter drop. "What do you mean, you'd jinx them?" he said.

"That's what I mean," I said. "If I bet on them, I'd jinx them." I couldn't explain it all to Elliot. I had always felt that the life of the Dodgers and my life were inextricably entwined. Up until that day I had always felt that they controlled my fate. Certainly what they did determined whether I was happy or sad. But now, now that I was in the ball park, I had the uncanny feeling that somehow I controlled *their* fate. I would not involve them in my own luck, which, after all, might not be any good.

Elliot would have pressed the point, but Davy put his hand on Elliot's arm. "Let Sam watch the game," he said. "Sam's never seen a game." So Elliot laid off me for a while.

First man up for the Cubs was Stan Hack. He never could hit Ralph Branca for anything, and he struck out, one, two, three. I cheered and so did everybody else. Everybody except Elliot.

Branca walked Peanuts Lowrey, but then he struck out Bill Nicholson and Phil Cavarretta. The Dodgers were off to a very good start. In the bottom half of the first inning, nothing much happened, but the top of the second, I noticed something real funny. Jackie was playing first base. Ralph MacGruder, who was the second guy up, hit a long single to center field. Ralph MacGruder was this rookie Cub who had this one good season and was never heard of again, and if you want to know the truth, that's just as well, because he slid into first base, where Jackie was standing with his foot on the pillow, ready to catch the ball. But Mac-Gruder didn't have to slide. There was no chance of Carl Furillo, out in center field, getting that ball to Jackie in time to tag MacGruder out. If that Mac-Gruder had been any kind of a ball player, he could have run that hit into a two-bagger. But he didn't. Instead he tried to spike Jackie. I saw it with my own eyes. He slid into first base. Jackie's back was to him, and MacGruder's foot went right for the back of Jackie's leg.

"Watch it, Jackie," I screamed. Someone—lots of people—much closer to Jackie than I was, must have screamed the same thing. Or maybe some instinct warned him. Anyway, he sidestepped and whirled around, leaving MacGruder lying there on the ground with his foot up in the air. He sure looked dumb. Jackie just shook his head and backed off, leaving MacGruder to get himself up as best he could.

"Did you see that? Did you see that?" I said to Davy.

"Yeah," Davy said. "I saw it."

"Don't you think they ought to take that MacGruder

out of the game now? That was against the rules. What he did there was against the rules."

"What did he do?" Davy asked me, a grim little smile on his usually cheerful face.

"He tried to spike Jackie. You saw it."

"Oh yes. I saw it and you saw it. But the umpires didn't see it. And as for Mr. MacGruder, he wasn't trying to spike Jackie. Oh, my goodness, no. He was just sliding into first base. And there's nothing illegal about sliding into first base, is there?"

I thought about that one for a long time. Actually for about an inning. Then Jackie Robinson hit his fifth home run of the season, knocking in Eddie Stanky too. I got so busy watching the ball game again that the whole incident slipped my mind, at least for the time being. The Dodgers won the first game 5-3. They also won the second game 4-3, but it took them ten innings to do it.

After the games were over, I remembered the spiking attempt. The four of us were still sitting in the nearly deserted stands. "No point in rushing," Davy said. "Nice sitting here with this breeze anyway. We wait a little bit, and we won't get tied up in all that traffic."

"Listen, Davy," I said. "Tell me now. What was that business with MacGruder and Jackie Robinson all about?"

"Now, Sam," Davy said slowly. "You know what it's all about. I explained it to you before. I told you what Branch Rickey said to Jackie."

"When Branch Rickey signed Jackie to be the first Negro big-league player in the history of baseball," I recited, "he told him he'd have to hold his temper, no matter how bad things got."

"What MacGruder did," Davy explained, "was one of the bad things. It's just one of the things the first Negro in baseball has got to put up with."

"That doesn't seem right," I said.

"Right?" Elliot laughed sharply. "There ain't nothing right about this whole damn life!"

"Why, Elliot," Davy said mildly, "the boy don't know much about that, and maybe it's just as well."

"Hey, Elliot," I said. "I'll bet with you next time the Giants play the Cards. You can have the Giants and I'll take St. Louis. Fifty cents. Even money. Even if they play at the Polo Grounds."

"It's a deal," Elliot said, holding out his hand. "Put 'er there." We shook on it.

After that we went to lots of ball games, sometimes the four of us, and sometimes just Davy and me in his old black Chevy. After the first time, Mom paid for my ticket. "It was O.K. for you to treat him the first time," Mom said to Davy. "In fact, it was wonderful of you.

And you can do it again sometime, for his birthday maybe. But he loves to go, and I'm so glad he has someone to take him. If you always paid, you couldn't take him so often. And we'll split the gas money and the tolls," she added.

"No, Mrs. Greene," Davy said. "No gas money."

"You gave Elliot gas and toll money," I said. "I saw you. If you can give it to Elliot, why can't I give it to you? Why can't we share expenses like that?"

Davy grinned at me. "O.K., Sam," he said. "You can pay half when it's just the two of us. When we go with Elliot, he and I'll take care of it."

So that's how it was. And if you want to know the truth, I preferred going with just Davy. I liked Elliot O.K., but Davy—well, he understood everything without my having to say it.

We went to Ebbets Field several other times that first summer, on Davy's days off and during his vacation. Somebody else took me to a game that summer too—Mr. Manheim, this customer at the inn, who went to the movies with my mother once in a while, and sometimes ate dinner with us. My mother must have told him I was going to these games with Davy so he said he and his friend Marty would take me to a night game one Friday. I had never been to a night game. That's why I said I'd go. Usually I didn't go places with people I hardly knew.

I shouldn't have gone that time, either. Mr. Manheim actually left before the game was over! It was the bottom of the eighth and the score was 7 to 0, favor of Brooklyn. Mr. Manheim said, "We might as well leave. There's no chance of the Cards winning, and this way we'll beat the traffic." What could I say? It was Mr. Manheim's car. I never went to a game with him again. He asked me lots of times, but I would never go. Davy would never do a thing like that. Mr. Manheim didn't get to Ebbets Field in time for batting practice either.

Batting practice was important. You got to see the players kind of relaxed and natural during batting practice, when there weren't too many people in the ball park, at least not at the beginning. We liked to watch all the Dodgers at batting practice because we liked to think about them as people, not just as ball players. We liked all the Dodgers. We liked Ralph Branca and Eddie Stanky and Gene Hermanski and Carl Furillo. We loved good old Pee Wee Reese. I guess Pee Wee was the soul of the Dodgers in those years. But the electric heart of the team was Jackie Robinson, and we followed his adventures daily like each one was a new chapter in a soap opera.

In the second game Davy took me to during his vacation, Pete Rieser hit a home run out of the ball park. I followed the ball with my eyes as it went over the right-field wall. It disappeared onto Bedford Avenue and all I could see was the laundry flapping on the apartment-house roofs across the street.

"I hope some kid is out there on Bedford Avenue," Davy said. "I hope some lucky kid finds that ball."

"Yeah," I said. "It would be great to have an actual ball that Pete Rieser hit. Or Jackie Robinson," I added hopefully. "Or any Dodger."

"Don't you know what happens to a kid who gets one of those balls that's hit over the right-field wall?"

"No," I said, "I never heard of it."

"Oh, sure you have," Davy protested. "Red Barber talks about them all the time."

"Oh, yeah," I said. I remembered hearing Red Barber talk about Old Gold Specials, but I had never known exactly what he had meant.

"The kid who finds that ball can get into the park for nothing," Davy said. "All he has to do is show it at the gate and they'll let him in. And then all the Dodgers will autograph the ball for him. Of course, they'll do that for anyone who catches a ball, even if it was just hit into the stands."

"Geez," I said, "I'd sure like to have one of those balls."

"We don't ever sit close enough to get one," Davy said. "If I had one, I'd put it into one of those glass cases, like the one Henrietta's got that clock in, and I'd put it on the coffee table in the living room."

"Hey," Henrietta said, "you aren't putting no dirty

old ball in my living room next to my German clock. Not when I just put up new wallpaper and got the whole place looking real good."

"Don't you worry about it none, Henrietta," Davy said. "I haven't got that ball yet. And if I did catch one, I'd look pretty dumb going down into the dugout to get it autographed, like a kid."

"Oh, I'd go down with you." I said. "You could pretend it was for me."

"Well, maybe I wouldn't pretend," Davy said. "Maybe it really would be for you. Yeah, that's right. If I caught a ball, I'd give it to you."

"Why?" I asked. "Why would you do that? You just said you'd like to have one."

"Well, yes, I would," Davy said. "Of course I would, but so would you."

That didn't seem to me to be much of an answer, so all I said was, "Well, if I catch one, I'll give it to you." And we let it go at that.

The season came to an end, as seasons do. The Dodgers won the National League Pennant, but they lost the World Series to the Yankees. Davy wasn't too discouraged. He said that before the Series began, there weren't three bookies in New York who'd have given you 7-1 odds the Series would go more than four games. After the Dodgers lost the first two, there wasn't even one bookie. But then the Dodgers forced the Yankees to go the whole seven games. They won the third game. They almost lost the fourth. Yankee pitcher Bill Bevens was on his way to the first no-hitter in World Series history, with two outs in the last of the ninth, when Cookie Lavagetto hit a double with men on first and second and the Dodgers won, 3-2. They lost the fifth, won the sixth, 8-6, in a nerve-racking contest at Yankee Stadium, and then lost the seventh.

Jackie Robinson was named Rookie of the Year.

Davy said, "Wait 'till next year. . . ."

But the next year wasn't so good. Actually, it was crummy. The Dodgers finished third.

It didn't look bad all the way, though. There were times when we could believe they were going to make it. You really couldn't count them out until September. So Davy and me, we had a good time, all summer long.

But the spring was lousy. They spent some of that spring in the cellar. The previous season's pennant-winners in the cellar! But that's what made life with the Dodgers exciting. They were completely unpredictable.

We were at Ebbets Field one night during that second spring, the spring of 1948, when the Chicago Cubs beat Brooklyn 4-1. It was really sickening, even

though the Cubs' pitcher, Johnny Schmitz, was probably tougher for the Dodgers to beat than any other
pitcher in the National League.

Jackie Robinson was having a bad beginning too.
Something was wrong with his knee and he was on the
bench almost as much as he was in the line-up all
through April and May. That night he did work a
double play with Harry Taylor, the Dodger pitcher.
Nothing seemed to dim his fielding ability, but he sure
wasn't hitting.

Davy and I talked about the game on the way home
in the car. It was late, but I was too depressed to
sleep. I never slept on the way home from night
games. If I wasn't too depressed, I was too excited.
Anyway, I loved driving home, just Davy and me, in
the dark, talking, even if the Dodgers had lost. Mother
thought I slept; that's the only reason she let me go to
night games during school.

I was looking for reasons why the Dodgers were
doing so badly. "I hate to say this," I remarked to
Davy, "but that Ebbets Field is a lousy ball park. It's
too small."

"What d'ya mean, too small?" Davy answered. "It's
the same ninety feet from first base to second in every
ball park. It's the same sixty feet from home plate to
the pitcher's mound."

"Oh, you know what I mean," I said impatiently.

"You know darn well not every ball park has such a short right-field line. They feel cramped in that park. Jackie feels cramped."

"Nonsense," Davy said. "You know that's nonsense. You know it may be easier to hit one out of Ebbets Field than just about anywhere else, in spite of that high right-field wall."

Davy was right, of course, but I was arguing for argument's own sake. "I don't know," I said grumpily. "When we saw Jackie at the Polo Grounds last season, he did terrific."

"Well, what we really ought to do," Davy responded judiciously, "is go watch the Dodgers play in some other ball parks."

"Yeah, you're right, Davy." I was all excited. "We ought to see what those other ball parks look like. We ought to get to know the fans in other towns." I wanted to be fair. Even though I was looking for excuses, I really wanted to be fair. I wanted to examine all the Dodgers from every angle, and if they had faults, to know those faults as well as their virtues. I wanted to know the totality of them as human beings. I wanted them to be real. Especially Jackie Robinson. Because when Jackie Robinson was having a bad time, the whole team seemed to be having a bad time.

Davy agreed with me. "That way we'll have a better idea of what our Dodgers are up against," he said.

51

So that's what we did. We made sort of a collection of ball parks.

We had already been to the Polo Grounds, and not only when the Dodgers were playing. We sometimes went there to a night game on our way home from Ebbets Field, just to see another ball game. Sometimes we went with Elliot, to keep him company. We didn't always have to watch the Dodgers.

And getting to Shibe Park in Philadelphia wasn't very hard either. What was hard was watching the Phillies play that year. They had to be about the lousiest ball club in either league and it was awful to waste the price of general admission to watch them. But at least we got to see what the inside of another ball park looked like. Or anyway, I did. Davy had been there before.

Once we actually drove all the way to Braves Field in Boston to see a night game. We left Winter Hill after lunch and we got to the ball park at seven. The game was over about 10:00 and we were not back in Winter Hill until four in the morning. It was a lot of driving, and Davy did it all himself.

The next day I staggered downstairs about noon and there was Davy, already at the big range, getting soups and stews and things ready for lunch. I'd like to say that he looked as fresh as usual, but if you want to know the truth, he didn't. He looked kind of pale, kind of ashy gray beneath his blackness, if you know what I mean. It was already 90 degrees in that kitchen and the day had hardly begun yet.

"I don't see how you made it in this morning, Davy," I said. "I'm exhausted and I didn't even drive."

"Didn't have much choice, did I?" Davy asked.

"You look kinda tired," I said. "Maybe we shouldn't have gone. Maybe it was a mistake."

"Don't ever regret what's done, boy," Davy said. "There's no point in that."

"But Jackie Robinson only played four innings," I moaned. "He didn't hit a single ball. He never even got on base."

"Ain't no player ever hit in 154 games," Davy said. "Not even Babe Ruth. Jackie worked another double play, and the Dodgers won. At least the Dodgers won. What if we'd driven all the way to Boston to see them lose?"

"Yeah," I admitted, "thank God they won. But Braves Field isn't much of a ball park either. It's a lot smaller than the Polo Grounds."

Davy nodded. "We got one more ball park to see," he said. "Forbes Field."

"Forbes Field!" I exclaimed. "But Pittsburgh is a million miles away."

"We'll go during my vacation," Davy said. "Elliott and Henrietta will come too, and share the driving.

Pittsburgh is about as far as we can go without having to sleep over somewhere, but it ain't no million miles."

For the next three weeks we planned that trip to Pittsburgh. My mother thought we had a couple of screws loose, and to be perfectly honest, I don't think Henrietta was any too crazy about the idea either. So that made only three of us who were nuts. Elliot was as keen on the idea as Davy and me. But Henrietta kept saying things like, "Pops, are you up to it? You know what the doctor said."

"The doctor said take it easy. Take it easy. Listen, Henrietta, if you have to go around all the time taking it easy, you might as well be dead. I believe that, Henrietta."

"Yeah, Pops," she said sadly, "I know you do."

"Every day all summer long I work in that kitchen in 100 degrees of heat. If I can stand that, I can sure manage to drive to Pittsburgh in Elliot's nice comfortable Oldsmobile with the breeze blowing in through the window."

Davy was sitting at the dining-room table nearest the kitchen door, drinking his iced coffee. Henrietta and I were drinking Cokes, and my mother had hot coffee. It didn't matter what the weather was, my mother always drank hot coffee.

"Maybe you could stay overnight some place," she said. She had given up trying to talk us out of it altogether. Somehow, somewhere, she had lost control of the situation.

"Well no, Mrs. Greene," Davy said. "I don't think we could do that. We're kind of a mixed group."

My mother nodded. "It was a dumb idea," she said. "I don't know why I mentioned it." She seemed a little embarrassed even.

"None of us could afford it anyway," Henrietta said. "This whole trip's going to cost a fortune in gas as it is."

"That's right," my mother agreed. "Nobody could afford it." She turned to me and tried once more, "Sam, for heaven's sake, what do you have to go to Pittsburgh for?"

"I told you, Mother," I repeated patiently, "to see the ball park. I got to see the ball park."

"And I suppose," she said to Davy, "you got to see the ball park too."

"Well, I'd sure like to," Davy said. "I'd sure like to see as many different ball parks as I could before I die."

"Maybe wait till next year," Henrietta said, "when you're feeling better."

"I'm feeling fine," Davy said. "Just fine. And you should never wait till next year if you can help it. Next year is a very chancy thing."

That seemed to shut Henrietta up, and we all went

to Pittsburgh without any more discussion. It was the most exciting day—or days—of my life. It was eerie, getting up at 1 A.M. after a few hours' sleep, and setting out in the black, damp warmth of the summer night. Davy hadn't slept at all. We left as soon as he was done working.

We drove almost in silence, because everyone except the driver would kind of doze off. And then all of a sudden there'd be this bright pool of light in the middle of the blackness, and that would be a gas station along the Pennsylvania Turnpike and we'd stop there for gas and to use the rest rooms. The gas-station attendant looked at us kind of funny when the four of us got out of the car, but we were used to that and didn't pay any attention. We got the same stares when we all sat down together in the bleachers at the ball park. No matter how much sun I got, I never tanned. I only turned red, and peeled, and ended up with more freckles than ever. That was how it was.

We couldn't stop at any restaurants to eat, so we carried plenty of food with us, including a big gallon Thermos of coffee to keep the drivers going. And then we stuffed ourselves on hot dogs and all that junk when we got to Forbes Field. We denied ourselves nothing. It was not just another trip to a ball game; it was a holiday, and for once we didn't care how much money we spent or how sick we might be after we got home. We were all on vacation.

The ball players didn't disappoint us either. The Dodgers won the first game, 7–6, and though they lost the second one, 7–4, even I had to admit that it was an exciting game. Jackie didn't hit any home runs. Actually, he never was one of these super long-ball hitters. He was what you might call the perfect all-around ballplayer. In the first game he hit a double, scored two runs, stole home and participated in two double plays, one unassisted. In the second game his performance was somewhat less spectacular, but he still scored a run, and made two put-outs and an assist. I was convinced at last that Jackie was the greatest ballplayer in the National League, wherever he played. Home-run hitting was the least of it. What Jackie could do he could do in any field, no matter how small or large.

Going home we were lots noisier than we had been coming out. Even though we'd driven for eleven hours and watched two ball games, we weren't tired. We were exhilarated. We sang, we joked. They made me recite all the games in the last two seasons in which the Dodgers had beaten the Pirates. I had bet with Elliot on the Giant-Cub game played that day in Chicago. The loser had to treat all the rest of us to ice cream. Elliot—and the Giants—lost, 6–3. When we stopped for gas, he gave me the money and I had to run into the Howard Johnson's next door to buy the cones. I didn't like going up to a counter because it always took the guy in back of it so long to notice me, but this time I had to. I finally got coffee ice cream for Davy and Elliot, butter pecan for Henrietta, and vanilla for myself. Actually, I could hardly swallow the ice cream after all the crap I'd stuffed myself with at Forbes Field, but I finished it to the last drop for Elliot's sake.

We got home at four in the morning, twenty-seven hours after we started out. That's why I said the best days of my life before, instead of day.

It was downhill all the way after that. All through the deep summer the Dodgers had fought the Braves, the Cards, the Pirates, and the Giants for the pennant, but when autumn came, the Braves clinched it pretty easily, and the Dodgers didn't even get second-place money. That went to the Cardinals.

Davy said, "Wait till next year."

"I thought you said next year is a very chancy thing," I reminded him.

"I said," Davy reminded me, "never wait till next year if you can help it. But if you can't help it, well, then, you've got to. Listen, Sammy," he added, "human beings live in hope. That's what the Dodgers taught me, all those lean years before the war. Wait till next year."

Next year came. It was Jackie Robinson's greatest year in the major leagues. Of course, we didn't know that when the season began. We didn't even know it when the season was over. That's the kind of thing you don't know till later, when you're looking back.

In July my sisters went for two weeks to Girl Scout camp. My mother wanted me to go to the Boy Scout camp across the lake, even though I didn't even belong to the Boy Scouts.

"That doesn't matter," she said. "You could join and they'd let you go to the camp. They play lots of baseball there."

"I don't want to go," I said.

"They swim. They sleep out. They'd let you bring your radio."

"I don't want to go," I repeated. "What would I eat?"

"They have egg salad there too," she said. "Besides, it's about time you learned to eat other food, and to mix with other people. You can't spend your life running away from strangers."

"This place is full of strangers," I said. "I see enough strangers right here any particular day of the week to last me my whole life."

"But you don't talk to them," my mother said. "At camp, you'd have to talk to them. There wouldn't be anyone else. It would be good for you. It would help you grow up."

This whole discussion took place while we were eating dinner one night at the table in the dining room nearest the kitchen door. Sara was reading while she was eating, as usual. When Sara had her nose in a book, a volcano could suddenly erupt exactly where she was sitting, and she wouldn't pay the slightest attention. But when she wanted to, she heard what was going on. This time she lifted her head and said briefly, "Mother, you can't send Sammy to camp. He'd come home with malnutrition, and his voice would have withered away entirely, from disuse. He's too stubborn to change. He'd die first."

"But that isn't realistic," Mother groaned. Mother was very realistic.

"I think maybe Sammy will get realistic when he gets older." Sara turned to me. "Won't you, Sammy?" she asked.

I shrugged.

"He's twelve now," my mother said. "How long do we have to wait?"

"Remember the time two years ago you went to Cathie Silverwood's wedding and left us with that friend of yours—the one Sammy didn't know—and Sammy went around all day with a paper bag on his head so she wouldn't look at him? Remember that? Sammy didn't eat a bite that whole day, not one bite."

"Yes," Mother said sadly, " I remember." After that, there was no more talk about my going to camp. I wished Sara hadn't brought up that business about the paper bag, but I was so grateful to her for talking Mother out of her wild idea about me and Boy Scout camp that I decided not to complain again about the way she cooked eggs for the rest of the school year. We only had two more weeks to go anyway.

Early in July the girls went to camp and I was able to spend nearly all my time with Davy. Other summers the four of us had to go down and spend days and days at a time with my grandmother because my mother said at the inn we didn't get any fresh air and sunshine, but just hung around in our pajamas until eleven o'clock in the morning like a bunch of bar flies. But with the girls gone, she kind of forgot about me, which wasn't too hard, because I made sure I stayed out of her way. She was busy anyway. Mr. Manheim had dropped out of the picture and she had a new boyfriend, Mr. Cranach. I liked him better than Mr. Manheim. He didn't have any silly ideas about being buddy-buddy with me. Once he found out I wasn't much for conversation, he didn't press me. He never offered to take me to a ball game. I was free to spend my time with Davy, the portable radio, and my big loose-leaf notebook. Once in a while, if the bar was empty, I could even watch a game on T.V. But that didn't happen very often. My mother didn't let us in the bar when customers were there.

Davy and I went to two ball games at Ebbets Field

on the Fourth of July. It wasn't exactly a double-header, but rather two separate games, one at ten-thirty, the other at three. We paid twice and stayed for both. In the first game Jackie Robinson hit a triple and stole a base. The Dodgers won 7-1. In the second game he stole twice, bringing his record for the year to twenty. And it was only July.

The big inning in the second game was the fifth, when the Dodgers scored five runs. Bruce Edwards and Carl Furillo both hit homers into the center-field bleachers, where we were sitting. Boy, was that exciting. Carl Furillo's was so close to us, I could see the man who caught it. Right away he got into a fight with the kid sitting next to him. I couldn't hear what they were saying, there was too much noise, but I could see that the kid wanted the ball in the worst way. The kid's father got into the act too. I guess the father thought that the other man had somehow stolen what was rightfully his kid's ball by reaching out after it with longer arms or something.

I said to Davy, "If it was you and me, that wouldn't happen."

"You're right," Davy said. "We'd go down to the dugout together to get it autographed."

In a flash of inspiration, I knew at last what we'd do with such a ball if we ever got one. "You'd keep it six months in your house and then I'd keep it six months," I said. "And we'd go on and on like that for as long as we lived, trading it off every six months."

"And when I die," Davy said, "it'd come to you for keeps. I'd say that in my will. I wouldn't let that Elliot get his fat paws on it."

"He wouldn't want it anyway." I laughed. "It would be a *Dodger* ball."

"It would be Jackie Robinson's ball," Davy said. "It would be a ball that Jackie Robinson had hit."

"Well," I replied judiciously, "we'd take it no matter

who hit it. I mean, I wouldn't care if it was Duke Snider or Roy Campanella that hit it."

"Yeah, but as long as we're dreaming," Davy said, "we might as well dream good. We might as well make that ball perfect."

The Dodgers won that second game easy, beating Philadelphia, 8–4, even though the Phils weren't the pushovers they'd been the year before. It's more exciting when the game is closer, but Davy and I had a swell time as always, and I'm glad the Dodgers won, because that was the last time I got to see a game with Davy. I'd have really savored every second of it if I'd known, but I guess it's just as well I didn't know. Because if I'd known I'd have *appreciated* that game, but I couldn't have *enjoyed* it, if you know what I mean.

That Sunday the girls came back from camp and the next week we went down to my grandmother's for four days. When it was time for us to come back home, my mother drove down to get us, which was kind of funny. Usually she let us come home on the bus. The trip on the bus only took about three quarters of an hour. Of course, there were only two busses a day, but that didn't matter to us. In the summer, we didn't have any appointments.

After we'd all eaten lunch, my mother said she

wanted me to come for a little walk with her. She wanted me to walk with her down to the stream that ran along the bottom of my grandmother's meadow.

Right away I knew something was wrong. The last time my mother had said she wanted to take me and Sara for a walk was five years before, and she'd told us then that our father was going to die. I hadn't believed her, but she was right, and he did die. I still remembered that walk and I had this sick feeling at the bottom of my stomach at the thought of another one. And this one just for me. Not for Sara too.

We walked away from the house, and my mother said, "It's some gorgeous day, isn't it, Sam?"

"Look, Mom," I answered, "don't drag this thing out. I know something's wrong. What is it?"

My mother nodded. She wasn't much of a one for beating around the bush either. "Davy's very sick," she said. "He had a heart attack. He's in the hospital."

The sick emptiness in my stomach grew larger. "Is this the first heart attack he's ever had?" I asked.

"No," my mother answered. "It's his second. He had one about a year before he came to us."

I heaved a sigh of relief. "It's the third one that kills you," I said.

"What makes you say that?" my mother asked.

"It was the third one that killed Dad."

"Well, maybe you're right," she said. "I hope so. He

seems to be resting pretty comfortably now, but it'll be several weeks before he can leave the hospital. I just wanted to tell you about it before we got home and you heard everyone else at the inn talking about it. I wanted you to hear it from me."

"O.K., Mother, thanks. I'll go see him as soon as I get home. It's a good thing I'm twelve now. They'll let me in. They would never let me in when Dad was sick. Not until that last day, anyway."

My mother shook her head. "I don't think they'll let you in this time either," she said. "Only immediate family. He's really very sick."

"Only immediate family? But all the immediate family he's got is Henrietta and Elliot. That's not enough!"

"His sister Evaline came up from North Carolina Wednesday. She'll probably stay around for a while."

"Oh, big deal," I answered angrily. "Some jerky sister from North Carolina who he probably hasn't seen in ten years."

"Knowing Davy," my mother said softly, "I'm sure he's quite fond of her."

I was looking for a real big stone to throw in the stream—one that would make one terrific splash. I found it and threw it in so hard that the spray hit me and my mother both. But she just brushed her dress off absentmindedly and didn't say anything about it.

"I can send him my radio," I said. "At least he can hear the ball games."

"Elliot wanted to get him a radio, but the doctor said nothing doing. He's not to have any excitement, and you know how excited you and he get over those games."

"But it'll be worse for him, worrying about how the Dodgers are doing."

"Oh, he can see the papers. Henrietta goes up each afternoon and reports to him."

"How about you?" I asked. "Did they let you go see him?"

"Well, I kind of snuck in," she answered.

I nodded, satisfied. If my mother had found a way to sneak in, a full-grown thirty-seven-year-old woman like her, a scrungy kid of twelve would surely find a way.

But being a scrungy kid of twelve is exactly what made it so impossible for me to get past that witch who sat at the desk in the front lobby of the hospital. She was no nurse or anything—just a volunteer, but the way she acted you'd think she was boss of the whole world. And I didn't look twelve, so if I managed to sneak in any of the other entrances to the hospital somebody was sure to stop me and ask me what I was doing there and politely, or not so politely depending on whether they were decent or mean, throw me out.

Decent or mean, it came to the same thing in the end.

It was pretty awful for me, having to talk to all those people I didn't know. I couldn't explain to them what I was doing in the hospital. It would have taken too many words to explain about me and Davy. Look how many it's taken me already, and actually, I haven't told the half of it.

My mother was no help. She did not approve of my trying to see Davy, and when I took that five-mile ride on my bike to the hospital I had to tell her I was going to play baseball in the schoolyard with Mickey and Al.

What really got me, though, was when Henrietta told me he was asking for me. I think she thought that would please me and make me feel better about not getting to see him, but it only made me feel worse. I had been hanging around that hospital for days, in the afternoon or evening—whenever there was no game on the radio. The news that he wanted to see me was the last straw. I'd had it. I was going to do something spectacular. I was going to make him better all by myself. It would be like magic.

I made my plans carefully. It would take quite a bit of money. I got twenty-five cents a week allowance, most of which I spent on baseball books and magazines, so I only had fifty cents saved up out of that. But I was due for another quarter on Friday, and that would make seventy-five cents. And then I had my birthday money. I had collected three dollars and fifty cents on my birthday in May and I hadn't spent any of it. Of course, it was downstairs in the safe, but my mother would give it to me if I told her I needed it to buy Davy a present. She would approve of that. Besides it was true.

I figured the whole deal would cost me about five-fifty and I had four twenty-five. I had to dig up another dollar and a quarter. Sara was the only possibility. Fran and Rosy were easier to con, but they only got ten cents a week each, which they spent instantly on candy and bubble gum, and their birthdays were in October and December, so anything they'd gotten at that time was long gone.

I looked out of my bedroom window, and sure enough, there was Sara, sitting on one of the white wooden chairs Cal the porter set out on the lawn during the summer. She was reading, naturally. I grabbed the latest issue of *Baseball* magazine, even though I'd read it through seven times already, and ran downstairs to join her.

I sat down in the chair next to her and opened my magazine. For a while I read busily. So did she. But I knew it wouldn't last long. I knew Sara. She couldn't stand to be around me for more than five minutes without lecturing me.

Exactly five minutes had passed when she started.

I figured that out from the sun. "You know, Sam," she said, "this is a very good book I'm reading. I think you'd like it."

"Yeah?" I said. I wanted to sound a little interested but not too interested. Since my usual reply to that opening gambit was, "Oh, dry up, for crissakes," anything more than "yeah" would surely arouse her suspicion.

She didn't need much encouragement. "Yeah?" was enough.

"It's called *The Count of Monte Cristo*," she said, "and it's very exciting. It's all about this man who's unjustly imprisoned and how he gets revenge on the people who framed him."

"I think I saw it in the movies," I said. "With James Cagney."

"It's not that kind of story," she said impatiently. "It's not a gangster story."

"It looks awful fat," I remarked. "Too fat for me to read."

"Remember when I made you read *The Wind in the Willows?*" she asked. "You liked that, didn't you?"

"It was all right," I said. "But that was two years ago. You can't expect me to go around reading about rats and toads now, can you?"

"*The Count of Monte Cristo* is a grown-up book. It was written for grown-ups."

"Besides," I pointed out. "I had to read *The Wind*

in the Willows. I needed it for a book report and Miss Frobisher said I couldn't read another sports story."

"Nobody has to *read* a book for a book report," she said firmly. "You must have liked it."

"I said it was all right. That's what it was—all right."

"This one you'd like. You'd really like it. I promise you."

"I've wasted more time on your promises," I said. "I need more than promises." I wanted the suggestion to come from her, but if she didn't make it, I was going to have to get to it soon myself.

"You don't like it," she offered, "and I'll give you my allowance for the next two weeks." Now we were getting somewhere. She made fifty cents a week. "I'll give you my allowance for one week even if you do like it. Just for reading it. I'll pay you fifty cents just for reading it."

"I have a better plan," I said. "With my plan, I can be sure I won't be wasting my time. Give me the dollar in advance. If I like the book, I'll give it back to you. All of it. You won't have to pay me anything if I like the book."

"How do I know you won't lie?"

"I could lie anyway. Under your plan I could have lied too. But I won't. You know I won't. I never do."

She nodded. She knew it was true. We, none of us, ever lied to each other. We might con each other. And we certainly lied occasionally to our mother and with perfect regularity to certain other dumb grown-ups. But we never lied to each other.

"All right," she said. "A dollar. When I'm finished with this book, I'll give it to you with a dollar."

An unexpected roadblock. "When do you think you'll be finished?"

"What difference does it make to you?"

I almost told a lie. I almost said, "So I won't start something else—so I won't start that new biography of Babe Ruth I got from the library." But instead I said, "I need the money."

"For what?"

"I can't tell you. Not now. Later."

She accepted that. "O.K., I'll give you the money now. You can have the book tomorrow probably. I see it's going to take me four weeks to get that dollar back."

"You may never get it back."

"Yes I will. You're going to love this book." She went upstairs to get me the money.

I was still short a quarter, but I decided to risk doing without it. I didn't have to eat hot dogs at the game. I could take a sandwich without embarrassment. I wasn't likely to run into anyone I knew.

Of course, this whole adventure was going to force me into an awful lot of conversation with people I'd never met. But I would manage that somehow. I had to.

That afternoon I got on my bike and rode downtown. I went into Muldoon's Sporting Goods and bought a brand new Spalding regulation baseball. It cost one sixty-five. I couldn't count on catching one at the ball park. In all the time we had gone to the games that had never happened to us. It probably never would, if we went to a thousand million games. I had to take matters into my own hands, and then rough the ball up a little bit and persuade the players to autograph it, even if I hadn't caught it.

The day after that was Friday. I collected my allowance and got my mother to give me the three dollars and fifty cents that was in the safe.

"I think that's too much to spend on a present for Davy," Mother said. "A dollar would be plenty."

"Mother!" I exclaimed. I was shocked. "If I had a thousand dollars it wouldn't be too much to spend."

"Davy wouldn't want you to spend all your money on him. You know that."

"*I* want to spend all my money on Davy," I said. "Davy never has to know."

"It's your money, but I think you're crazy. You don't need to spend money to show love."

"It's the only way," I said. "They won't let me in to see him."

"It's your money," she repeated, shaking her head, but then she gave it to me.

The next day, Saturday, was of course the busiest day of the week at the inn. Even during July and August, the slow months, Saturday was sometimes busy. I was lucky. On this particular Saturday there was a wedding reception. What with Davy sick and the new cook not quite up to preparing a whole banquet, my mother had to be in six places at once. She really didn't have time to worry about us. It was one of those days when she just wanted us to disappear somewhere and not bother her until it was time for Sara and me to help dish out the meal. I obliged. I told her I was going over to Mickey's house and that I would stay there for dinner, but I'd come home before dark. If she had time to think about it, she might have wondered why I spent so much time at Mickey's lately, but she didn't have time to think about it. "Rosy can put the gravy on the turkey," I said. "She's big enough."

My mother nodded absently. "Have fun," she said and hurried off.

I suppose I could have told her where I was going. She might have been perfectly willing to let me go. She might have given me money for it. But I couldn't be sure. A mother who worried so much about our crossing the highway after sunset might not want us to go all the way to Ebbets Field by ourselves. I couldn't risk her telling me not to go. So I just went. It was different in those days. No one worried about drug addicts or getting mugged in the subway or anything like that.

I had gone into the kitchen real early in the morning, before anyone else was up, and made myself a couple of egg-salad sandwiches. I had them and my money and the baseball in its little cardboard box. I walked the mile and a half to the bus station because there'd be no place to leave my bike if I rode there. I took the bus into New York City and I took a subway to Ebbets Field. I didn't have to ask anyone anything except the bus driver for a ticket to New York City and the man in the subway booth for change of a quarter. There was one thing I'd learned from Sara, and that was that if you know how to read you can do anything. Right in the middle of the subway was this big map of the subway system and Ebbets Field was marked right on it in large black letters. BMT, Brighton Local, downtown, get off at the station near Ebbets Field. I didn't even have to change trains.

You could see flags flying above the ball park when you climbed up out of the subway station. You had to walk three blocks and there you were. Inside it was as it always had been, as bright and green as ever, remote from the sooty streets that surrounded it, remote from all the world. In the excitement of being there, I almost forgot about Davy for a moment. I almost forgot why I had come. But then, when the Cubs' pitcher, Warren Hacker, began to warm up, I turned to Davy to ask him if he thought Shotton was going to give Jackie's sore heel a rest that day, but Davy wasn't there, and I remembered.

I thought maybe I'd better start trying right away. My chances were probably better during batting practice than they would be later. I took my ball out of its box and stashed the box underneath my bleacher seat. Then I walked around to the first-base side and climbed all the way down to the box seats right behind the dugout. I leaned over the rail. Billy Cox was trotting back to the dugout from home plate, where Erskine had been throwing to him.

I swallowed my heart, which seemed to be beating in my throat, and called out, "Billy, hey Billy," waving my ball as hard and high as I could. But I was scared, and my voice wasn't very loud, and I don't think Billy Cox heard me. He disappeared into the dugout.

Marv Rackley came out of the dugout and then Carl Furillo. I called to them too, but they didn't seem to hear me either.

This method was getting me nowhere. I had to try something else before the game began and I'd really lost my chance. I looked around to see if there were any ushers nearby, but none was in sight. It was kind of early and the place hadn't really started to fill up yet. I guess the ushers were loafing around the refreshment stands, smoking cigarettes.

I climbed up on the railing and then hoisted myself onto the roof of the dugout. That was something you could not do at many places besides Ebbets Field. That was one of the few advantages of such a small ball park. Of course, you know, you couldn't go see Ebbets Field now if you wanted to. They tore it down and put an apartment building there.

I could have stood up and walked across the dugout roof to the edge, but I figured if I did that an usher surely would see me. I sneaked across the roof on my belly until I came to the edge and then I leaned over.

It was really very nice in the dugout. I had always kind of pictured it as being literally dug out of the dirt, like a trench in a war. But it had regular walls and a floor and benches and a water cooler. Only trouble was, there were just a couple of guys in there— Eddie Miksis, and Billy Cox whom I'd seen out on the field a few minutes before. I was disappointed. I had certainly hoped for Campy's signature, and Gil Hodges', and Pee Wee Reese's, and of course Jackie Robinson's. But I figured Davy would be thrilled with Miksis and Billy Cox, since their names on a ball

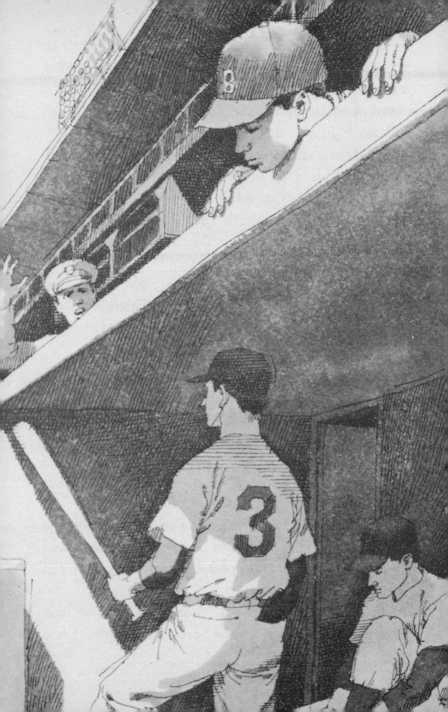

would be more than he'd ever expected. And anyway a few more guys might come meandering in before I was through.

But no matter how hard I swallowed, my heart was still stuck in my throat. "Eddie," I called. "Eddie, Billy." Hardly any sound came out of my mouth at all.

And then all of a sudden I heard a voice calling real loud. Whoever it was didn't have any trouble getting the sound out of *his* mouth. "Hey you, kid, get down off that roof," the voice said. "What do you think you're doing?" I sat up and turned around. An angry usher was standing at the foot of the aisle, right by the railing, screaming at me. "Get yourself off that roof," he shouted. "Right now, or I'll throw you out of the ball park."

I scrambled down fast as I could. Boy, was I a mess. My chino pants and my striped jersey were absolutely covered with dust and grime from that roof. I guess my face and arms weren't any too clean either. I looked like a bum.

"I'm going to throw you out anyway," the usher said, "because you don't have a ticket."

I got real mad when I heard him say that. People had been throwing me out of places all week long and I was plenty sick of it. Especially since I certainly did have a ticket.

"You can't throw me out," I shouted back at him. "I've got as much right to be here as you have." I had suddenly found my voice. I was scared of the ball players, but this usher didn't frighten me one bit. I pulled my ticket stub out of my pocket. "See?" I said, thrusting it into his face, "I certainly do have a ticket."

He made as if to take it out of my hand. I guess he wanted to look at it close, to make sure it was a stub from that day and not an old one I carried around in my pocket for emergencies. But I pulled my hand back.

"Oh, no, you don't," I said. "You can't take this ticket away from me. You won't give it back to me and then you'll throw me out because I don't have a ticket!"

"You crazy, kid?" he asked, shaking his head. "This is what I get for working in Ebbets Field. A bunch of crazy people. Next year I'm applying for a job at the Polo Grounds."

"Go, ahead," I said, "you traitor. Who needs you?" I turned away from him and leaned over the rail.

"I better not see you on that roof again," the usher said. "I'll have my eye out for you—and so will all the other ushers."

"Don't worry," I said.

Then I felt his hand on my shoulder. "As a matter of fact, kid," he said, "I think I'll escort you to your seat where you belong. Up in the bleachers where you can't make any trouble!"

Well, right then and there the whole enterprise

would have gone up in smoke if old Jackie Robinson himself had not come trotting out onto the field from the dugout that very second. "Hey, Jackie," I called, "Hey, Jackie," in a voice as loud as a thunderbolt. I mean there were two airplanes flying overhead right that minute and Jackie Robinson heard me anyway.

He glanced over in the direction he could tell my voice was coming from, and I began to wave frantically, still calling "Jackie, hey, Jackie."

He lifted up his hand, gave one wide wave, and smiled. "Hey, kid," he called, and continued on his way to the batting cage. In another instant he'd have been too busy with batting practice to pay any attention to me.

"Sign my ball," I screamed. "Sign my ball."

He seemed to hesitate briefly. I took this as a good omen. "You gotta," I went on frantically. "Please, please, you gotta."

"He don't gotta do nothing," the usher said. "That's Jackie Robinson and everyone knows that he don't gotta do nothing."

I went right on screaming.

"Come on, kid," the usher said, "we're getting out of here." He was a big hulking usher who must have weighed about eight hundred pounds, and he began pulling on me. Even though I gripped the cement with my sneakers and held onto the rail with my hand, he managed to pull me loose. But he couldn't shut me up.

"Please, Jackie, please," I went right on screaming.

It worked. Or something worked. If not my scream-ing, then maybe the sight of that monster usher trying to pull me up the aisle and scrungy old me pulling against him for dear life.

"Let the kid go," Jackie Robinson said when he got to the railing. "All he wants is an autograph."

"He's a fresh kid," the usher said, but he let me go.

"Kids are supposed to be fresh," Jackie Robinson said.

I thrust my ball into Jackie's Robinson's face. "Gee, thanks, Mr. Robinson," I said. "Sign it, please."

"You got a pen?" he asked.

"A pen?" I could have kicked myself. "A pen?" I'd forgotten a pen! I turned to the usher. "You got a pen?"

"If I had," the usher said triumphantly, "I certainly wouldn't lend it to you!"

"Oh, come on," Jackie Robinson said, "don't be so vindictive. What harm did the kid do, after all?"

"Well, as it happens, I don't have one," the usher replied smugly.

"Wait here," I said. "Wait right here, Mr. Robin-son. I'll go find one."

Jackie Robinson laughed. "Sorry, kid, but I've got work to do. Another time, maybe."

"Please, Mr. Robinson," I said. "It's for my friend. My friend, Davy."

"Well, let Davy come and get his own autographs," he said. "Why should you do his dirty work for him?"

"He can't come," I said. The words came rushing out of me, tumbling one on top of the other. I had to tell Jackie Robinson all about it, before he went away. "Davy can't come because he's sick. He had a heart attack."

"A heart attack?" Jackie Robinson asked. "A kid had a heart attack?"

"He's not a kid," I explained. "He's sixty years old. He's my best friend. He's a colored man, like you. He's always loved the Dodgers, but lately he's loved them more than ever."

Now that I think about it, what I said could have annoyed Jackie Robinson very much. But at the time, it didn't. I guess he could tell how serious I was about what I was saying. "How did this Davy get to be your best friend?" he asked.

So I told him. I told him everything, or as near to everything as I could tell in five minutes. I told him how Davy worked for my mother, and how I had no father, so it was Davy who took me to my first ball game. I told him how they wouldn't let me into the hospital to see Davy, and how we had always talked about catching a ball that was hit into the stands and getting it autographed.

Jackie listened silently, nodding every once in a

while. When I was done at last, he said, "Well, now, kid, I'll tell you what. You keep this ball you brought with you. Keep it to play with. And borrow a pen from someone. Come back to the dugout the minute, the very second, the game is over, and I'll get you a real ball, one we played with, and I'll get all the guys to autograph it for you."

"Make sure it's one you hit," I said.

What nerve. I should have fainted dead away just because Jackie Robinson had deigned to speak to me. But here he was, making me an offer beyond my wildest dreams, and for me it wasn't enough. I had to have more. However, he didn't seem to care.

"O.K.," he said, "*if* I hit one." He had been in a little slump lately.

"You will," I said, "you will."

And he did. He broke the ball game wide open in the sixth inning when he hit a double to left field, scoring Rackley and Duke Snider. He scored himself when the Cubs pitcher, Warren Hacker, tried to pick him off second base. But Hacker overthrew, and Jackie, with that incredible speed he had, ran all the way home. Besides, he worked two double plays with Preacher Roe and Gil Hodges. On consecutive pitches, Carl Furillo and Billy Cox both hit home runs, shattering the 1930 Brooklyn home-run record of 122 for a season. The Dodgers scored six runs, and they scored them all in the sixth inning. They beat the Cubs, 6–1. They were hot, really hot, that day and that year.

But I really didn't watch the game as closely as I had all the others I'd been to see. I couldn't. My mind was on too many other things—on Jackie Robinson, on what was going to happen after the game was over, on that monster usher who I feared would yet find some way of spoiling things for me, but above all on Davy and the fact that he was missing all of the excitement.

And then I had to worry about getting hold of a pen. You could buy little pencils at the ball park for keeping box scores, but no pens. It was the first—and last—time in my life I walked into a ball park without something to write with. And I didn't see how I could borrow one from someone, since in all that mess of humanity I'd never find the person after the game to return it to him. Unless I took the guy's name and address and mailed it back to him later.

It didn't look to me like the guys in the bleachers where I was sitting had pens with them anyway. Most of them had on tee shirts, and tee shirts don't have pockets in them for pens. I decided to walk over to the seats along the first-base line to see if any of those fans looked more like pen owners. I had to go in that direction anyway to make sure I was at the dugout the second the ball game ended. I took with me my ball in its box.

On my way over I ran into this guy hawking Cokes and I decided to buy one in order to wash down the two egg-salad sandwiches I had eaten during the third inning.

This guy had a pen in his pocket. As a matter of fact he had two of them. "Look," I said to him, as I paid him for my soda, "could I borrow one of those pens?"

"Sure," he said, handing it to me after he had put my money into his change machine. He stood there, waiting, like he expected me to hand it back to him after I was done with it.

"Look," I said again, "maybe I could sort of buy it from you."

"Buy it from me? You mean the pen?"

"Yeah."

"What do you want my pen for?"

"I need it because Jackie Robinson promised me that after the game he and all the other guys would autograph a ball for me." Getting involved in all these explanations was really a pain in the neck.

"You don't say," the hawker remarked. I could tell he didn't believe me.

"It's true," I said. "Anyway, are you going to sell me your pen?"

"Sure. For a dollar."

I didn't have a dollar. Not any more. I'd have to try something else. I started to walk away.

"Oh, don't be silly, kid," he called to me. "Here, take the darn pen. Keep it." It was a nice pen. It was shaped like a bat, and on it, it said, "Ebbets Field, Home of the Brooklyn Dodgers."

"Hey, mister, thanks," I said. "That's real nice of you." It seemed to me I ought to do something for him, so I added, "I think I'd like another Coke." He sold me another Coke, and between sipping first from one and then from the other and trying to watch the game, I made very slow progress down to the dugout. I got there just before the game ended in the top of the ninth. The Dodgers didn't have to come up to bat at all in that final inning, and I was only afraid that they'd all have disappeared into the clubhouse by the time I got there. I should have come down at the end of the eighth. But Jackie Robinson had said the end of the game. Although my nerve had grown by about seven thousand per cent that day, I still didn't have enough to interrupt Jackie Robinson during a game.

I stood at the railing near the dugout, waiting, and sure enough, Jackie Robinson appeared around the corner of the building only a minute or two after Preacher Roe pitched that final out. All around me people were getting up to leave the ball park, but a lot of them stopped when they saw Jackie Robinson come to the rail to talk to me. Roy Campanella, Pee Wee Reese, and Gil Hodges were with him.

"Hi, kid," Jackie Robinson said. He was carrying a ball. It was covered with signatures. "Pee Wee here had a pen."

"And a good thing, too," Pee Wee said, "because most of the other guys left the field already."

"But these guys wanted to meet Davy's friend," Jackie Robinson said.

By that time, Preacher Roe had joined us at the railing. Jackie handed him the ball. "Hey, Preacher," he said, "got enough strength left in that arm to sign this ball for Davy's friend here?"

"Got a pen?" Preacher Roe asked.

I handed him the pen the hawker had given me. I was glad I hadn't gone through all the trouble of getting it for nothing.

"Not much room left on this ball," Roe said. He squirmed his signature into a little empty space beneath Duke Snider's and then he handed me both the pen and the ball. Everybody was waving programs and pens in the faces of the ball players who stood by the railing. But before they signed any of them, they all shook my hand. So did Jackie Robinson. I stood there, clutching Davy's ball and watching while those guys signed the programs of the other fans. Finally, though, they'd had enough. They smiled and waved their hands and walked away, five big men in white uniforms, etched sharply against the bright green grass. Jackie Robinson was the last one into the

dugout and before he disappeared around the corner, he turned and waved to me.

I waved back. "Thank you, Jackie Robinson," I called. "Thanks for everything." He nodded and smiled. I guess he heard me. I'm glad I remembered my manners before it was too late.

When everyone was gone, I looked down at the ball in my hands. Right between the rows of red seaming, Jackie Robinson had written, above his own signature, "For Davy. Get well soon." Then all the others had put their names around that.

I took the ball I had bought out of the box and put it in my pocket. I put the ball Jackie Robinson had given me in the box. Then I went home.

On Sundays Henrietta didn't have to go to Mrs. Martin's house where she worked, so I knew she'd get over to the hospital first thing. For the second morning in a row I was up and dressed and out of the inn while half the world was still eating breakfast. I rode my bike down to Witherspoon Street. When Henrietta answered the door I knew I'd figured right. She was all dressed, ready to go out. Elliot was sitting on the couch in a pair of old shorts reading the funnies. It was hot already.

Henrietta was surprised to see me. She asked me in. "Only you can't stay too long," she said. "I want to get over to the hospital to see Pops."

"That's why I came so early," I said, stepping into the living room and shutting the screen door behind me. "I wanted to catch you before you left. I have a present here for Davy. I want you to give it to him."

"Thanks very much, Sam," she answered. "That's very nice of you."

By this time, Elliot had put down his paper and come to stand beside her. He looked at the box I handed to Henrietta. I hadn't wrapped it or anything. "A ball?" Elliot asked in amazement. "Are you giving Davy a ball?"

"Whatever it is," Henrietta said hastily, "it's very nice of Sam. Very, very nice."

"It's a ball," I answered Elliot, "but not like you think. Go ahead, open it. You can look at it."

Elliot took the box from Henrietta and opened it. He lifted the ball out, his eyes growing wide with surprise. "Wow-eee," he said. "This is some ball! How'd you get it, Sammy? Steal it from some little kid—like Branch Rickey's grandson?"

"Elliot!" Henrietta scolded. "You don't even know if Branch Rickey has a grandson."

"It's all right, Henrietta," I said. "I know when Elliot's kidding. You didn't look at it closely enough, Elliot," I said to him. "Read what it says right here." I pointed to the writing between the rows of stitching.

"'For Davy,'" Elliot read. "'Get well soon. Jackie

Robinson.'" He shook his head. "My God, Sammy," he said, "this is some present. What did you have to do to get it?"

So I told him. When I was done, he said, "Henrietta, you can't give this ball to Davy. You have to let Sammy do it himself."

"I'd like to," Henrietta said, "but I—" she hesitated. "I don't think I should. I don't think we should wait until Pops get home to give him the ball."

"Oh, I didn't mean wait until he came home," Elliot said. "I meant find a way to get Sammy in there."

"They hardly want to let *you* in," Henrietta said. "Only immediate family. I don't think we can pass Sam off as immediate family." She laughed a small dry laugh.

"Leave it to me," Elliot said.

Henrietta looked at him doubtfully. "Look here, Elliot," she said, "I don't want you doing anything we'll all regret later." But she didn't sound as if she really meant it. I think she really wanted me to get in to see Davy.

"Don't you worry about it none," Elliot said to Henrietta. "It's something I'll take care of, and you don't have to know a thing about it. You just run along to the hospital now. Sammy can wait here while I go get dressed. You take the Oldsmobile. Sammy and I'll come over in Davy's Chevy."

"That's all right," Henrietta said. "I can take the Chevy."

"You'd get to hell in a handbasket sooner than you'd get across the street in that bucket," Elliot said. "Now, you do like I say, and no arguments."

Henrietta didn't answer Elliot back. She looked at me for a second, and then gave me a little hug. "See you later," she said, and then she left.

"Did you have any breakfast?" Elliot asked me after she was gone.

I shook my head. It had never occurred to the cook who had replaced Davy to offer me pancakes on a Sunday morning. I'd left the inn before he'd come in anyway.

Elliot sat me down at the kitchen table with a bowl of cornflakes, a glass of milk, and some peaches. Then he went upstairs to get dressed. I swallowed that whole bowl of cornflakes, even though cornflakes were not on the list of things that I would eat, because I didn't want to insult Elliot by not eating the breakfast he'd gotten for me. The peach was good, though.

By the time I was done, Elliot had come back down stairs. He had changed out of his old shorts, but he didn't have on his own clothes. He had on one of Davy's white chef's uniforms. He looked like a snowman in a January thaw. Three of Elliot could have fit into one of Davy's suits. I couldn't help laughing when I saw him.

"Oh, so you think I look funny, do you?" he asked me as he picked the car keys up from the table by the front door. He had to lift up the whole shirt in order to find the pants pocket to stick them in because he had pulled so much of the pants in with his belt, so they wouldn't fall down, that the top part was all out of shape. The pocket was all the way around in front.

"Yeah, I think you look funny," I said. "You look like you spent all your money buying a Good Humor truck and you haven't got any left for the suit."

"Nah, you got it all wrong," Elliot replied. "Can't you tell the difference between a Good Humor man and a laundry man when you see one?"

"Oh, so you've gone into the laundry business, have you?" I asked. "What happened to your job down at Steinhauer's Olds?"

"I'm only a laundry man for today," Elliot answered. "So come on, kid, let's get out of here before some other guy gets the laundry there ahead of me."

"Laundry men don't come on Sunday," I said.

"This one does. Only on Sunday." He opened the front door. "Come on," he repeated.

I followed him out of the house and into the old black Chevy. "What is this all about?" I asked.

"Oh, you'll see when we get there," Elliot said. "It's a very good idea. I'm really brilliant."

He was brilliant with the car, anyway. He managed to gentle it over to the hospital, even though it coughed and sputtered the whole ten minutes it took us to get there. He didn't tell me any more. He had to concentrate on driving. The car was on its last legs, the poor old thing. I kept thinking about the good times me and Davy had had in that old car, driving to and from ball games, singing and laughing and analyzing the whole way.

When we got to the hospital, Elliot parked the car near the entrance to the clinic. "If you think I can get in this way," I said, "you're wrong. I've tried it, three different times, and I've gotten tossed out three different times."

"Getting in is not your problem," Elliot said. "All you have to do to get in is walk through the door. It's staying in that's giving you trouble." He got out of the car, and as he slammed the door he said, "You just wait right here. I'll be back for you in a couple of minutes."

I wanted to know how long was a couple of minutes.

"Maybe three, maybe fifteen," Elliot said. "It all depends. You just wait."

So I waited. I got out of the car because it was so

hot, and I waited, leaning up against the door. By the time Elliot came back more than three minutes had passed, but less than fifteen. He was pushing a laundry cart—you know, one of those big canvas bags, hung on a frame with wheels. I looked inside. On the bottom were a couple of dirty, wrinkled old sheets.

"Get in," Elliot said. "Go ahead, get in."

"You mean," I said, light dawning in my thick skull at last, "I'm the laundry?"

"That's right, you're the Sunday laundry. But just to make sure, you'll cover your head with those sheets down there, and anyone who sees us will think I'm the newest orderly, picking up the dirty linen."

I made a face. "God knows," I said, "what kind of horrible disease the people who slept on those sheets have. Maybe leprosy. Maybe T.B. and they spit blood up all over them." We had seen a movie in health class about T.B.

"I'm sorry," Elliot said, his voice heavy with sarcasm. "I didn't know you were such a dainty gentleman. I would have gotten you some clean sheets, but they keep them locked up. The dirty ones are just in bundles on the floor of the linen room, with the carts."

"How did you know?" I asked. "How did you know where to get this stuff?"

"My friend Obie told me. Obie works here." He reached down into the bag and pulled the dirty sheets out. "Look here," he said, "are you going to get into this bag or not? Because if you're not, just give me that there ball and I'll take it up to Davy myself."

"I'm getting in, I'm getting in," I said hastily. I tipped the cart over and climbed in. Elliot righted it. As he leaned over to arrange the sheets on top of me, I managed to look up at him. "Thanks," I said. "Thanks a lot, Elliot." I wasn't being sarcastic. And Elliot knew I wasn't.

He shrugged. "That's O.K." he said. Then he added with a laugh, "I always knew you'd end up at the bottom of a pile of dirty laundry. Where can you go from here but up?" After that he threw the sheets on top of me and wheeled me across the parking lot.

That was some bumpy ride. I was small, but not really small enough for a laundry cart. Not soft enough, either. I was doubled over like a pretzel and still I hardly fit. Besides, the cart didn't have a hard bottom. It was only a bag. My rear end just about scraped the ground. I was afraid the whole time I was in that cart that the seam would bust and I'd end up sliding out of the darn thing before the very eyes of the witch who guarded the front door.

It didn't happen, though. Elliot wheeled me through the clinic entrance and down the corridor to the service elevator. The elevator was better. At least I wasn't bumping around. But it was crowded, and I didn't get very much air anyway, under those crummy sheets. So I started worrying about smothering to death.

Somebody in the elevator began talking to Elliot. "Are you new here?" she asked in one of those sunny voices old people sometimes put on when they're talking to kids. Only Elliot wasn't a kid.

"Yeah, that's right," he replied shortly.

"What do you do?"

"Well, I'm a new orderly," he said.

"My goodness, help changes around here so much, I can't hardly keep up with it. You're the fifth new orderly I've met this week. It's terrible the way you people keep coming and going, so irresponsible. I hope you're planning to stay with us a little while."

"Don't count on it," Elliot said.

"You won't last long," she said with a high little laugh, "if you take the dirty linen upstairs. It belongs downstairs."

"Gee, ma'am, thanks a lot," Elliot replied in a real humble voice. By this time the elevator had stopped at our floor and he had begun to wheel me out. "But I don't have any dirty laundry in this cart," he continued.

"Oh no?" the lady called. "Then what do you carry in a laundry cart?"

"Oh, just a corpse," Elliot said. I heard the woman

100

gasp. Then the elevator doors slammed shut and Elliot began to laugh. He laughed inside of himself all the way down the hall, until he stopped the cart. He waited a few minutes, and I heard footsteps moving past us. After the sound had completely died away, he lifted the sheets off me, and tipped the cart over.

"My God," I said, climbing out, "if you'd waited five minutes longer, I really would have been a corpse."

"Good," Elliot said. "Then I'd have found that dumb Dora and showed you to her. Would have served her right."

I sort of stretched my arms and legs to get the kinks out of them. "You were pretty good, Elliot," I said in a dignified voice, patting him on the back and making my face long and serious. "You handled that whole thing very well. I was proud of you."

Elliot laughed again. "That's enough now, kid," he said. "Get your rear end through that door." He pointed to the room just beyond where we were standing. "If someone else comes along and finds you in the hall, there'll be more questions to answer."

The door to the room stood open. "Aren't you coming?" I asked.

"Go on in alone," Elliot whispered. "The nurse'll throw one of us out if she finds three people standing by Davy's bed, and that one'll probably be you. If we obey the rules, maybe she won't notice."

I had to laugh at that remark about obeying the rules, but I guess Elliot was right. If you're driving a car full of money you stole from a bank, you're crazy if you go through any red lights.

I tiptoed quietly into the room. It was hot and sunny in there. White curtains hung limply at the one open window. There were four beds with men in all of them, but I hardly noticed them as I went softly by.

I could see Henrietta sitting in a wooden armchair with green plastic cushions next to the bed by the window. Davy lay in the bed. His eyes were shut. For a second I thought maybe he was dead already, but when I got closer I could see the white sheet moving with his shallow breath.

Maybe he wasn't dead, but he sure didn't look like Davy. He made such a small lump under that white sheet for a man who a few weeks before must have weighed more than two hundred pounds. And his face was kind of sunken and dull-looking, not round and shiny the way I was used to seeing it.

There was a smell in that room I didn't like. I had smelled that smell the day my father died, the day they had let us come into his hospital room to see him. All I could remember of that visit was the smell. I'd forgotten all the rest.

I really couldn't believe the man in the bed was Davy, even though I knew it was. He was not my Davy. He was not the Davy I wanted to know.

I was overcome with an almost irresistible desire to turn and run out of that room. I wanted to run as fast as my legs would carry me. It took the most tremendous effort of will to prevent my body from doing what it wanted to do. Luckily, my will had gotten some good training in the past couple of days. I had come this far, I had come through so much, I knew I couldn't go back again. So I just kind of looked at Henrietta, and she smiled at me and said, "It's O.K., Sammy, you can talk to him. He isn't really asleep—just dozing." I was shocked to hear her voice. She talked right out loud—she didn't even whisper, and her voice didn't even sound sad, the way it had in her house earlier that morning. It didn't sound particularly happy either—just normal. "Go ahead," she went on. "Go stand up there by the head of the bed and talk to him."

I did as she said. The top of the bed had been cranked up a little bit and I bent over the pillow. "Davy," I said softly, "Davy." My voice kind of cracked, so I repeated his name again, louder. "Davy, it's me, Sammy. I've brought you a present."

Even before his eyes opened—it seemed to cost him a great effort to open his eyes—his lips formed a little smile. I knew he had heard me. Then, his eyes did open and the smile got broader. He looked more like himself. His cheeks were still sunken and his skin still dull and loose, but his eyes and his smile were the same.

He spoke softly, in a kind of whisper, and very slowly, but with perfect clarity. "Why, boy, I am glad to see you. I sure am glad to see you."

I put my hand on his. "How do you feel?" I asked.

"Lots better," he said. "Nothing hurts me anymore. I'm just kinda tired. Once I have a little more energy they're going to let me go home."

"You been following the games O.K.?" I asked.

"Henrietta gives me the report every afternoon," Davy replied. "Sometimes I can even read the paper a little. They won't let me have a radio, you know. The doctor said it might disturb the other guys in the room."

"We been doing all right," I said.

"All right?" he said. "Just all right?" His voice got a little stronger. "My God, Sammy," he said, "this is the year we've been waiting for. This is next year! They won't blow it now."

"Don't get your hopes up," I said. Now I was talking to him like he usually talked to me. Now I was the old man and he was the boy. "You never can tell with the Dodgers. You can't count on the pennant until it's actually flying over the field."

"Nah," he said. "They won't blow it. This time they won't blow it."

"Well," I agreed carefully, "Jackie is sure having some season. I guess nothing can change that. It's already happened. He's so far ahead in batting he'd have to go into a terrible slump for anyone to catch up."

"It isn't just the hitting though," Davy said. We were going over the old ground again. "He can do everything. How many bases has he stolen this year so far?"

"Twenty-nine," I said. "And four times he stole home!"

"That's what I mean. And RBI's? How many RBI's?"

"A hundred and one," I said with a little laugh.

Davy almost crowed, even though he could speak only in that hoarse kind of whisper. "He can do anything," Davy said. "That boy can do anything."

"He sent you a present," I said.

Davy lifted his head and shoulders up sharply. "What are you talking about?" he said, almost in his old way. "Who sent me a present?"

"Jackie Robinson," I replied with a smile that came right up out of the inside of me. "Jackie Robinson himself, and all the Dodgers."

I put the box on the bed next to him.

"Crank me up a little more," he said. "I gotta see what you've got here."

Henrietta did it, and when he was comfortable he said, "Now, give me that there box." I did, and he opened it. He took out the ball. "Hand me my glasses," he ordered. "They're over there on the night stand." I obeyed, and then waited while he examined the ball for many minutes without saying a word. The men in the other beds were talking to their visitors, and I could hear the murmur of their voices, but it seemed to me as if Davy and Henrietta and I were floating on our own island of silence, far away from anyone else.

Finally he looked away from the ball which he had been turning and turning in his hands and looked at me. "How'd you come by this ball, Sammy?" he asked. "Did you finally catch an Old Gold Special?"

"Well, not exactly," I admitted. "But it turned out even better than that. That's a ball that Jackie Robinson himself hit. He hit a double with it." And then I told him the whole story of the day before.

Davy shook his head in wonder. "You went and did all that?" he said.

"Does your Mama know?" Henrietta asked. "Does your Mama know where you were and what you were doing yesterday?"

"Not yet," I admitted, "but don't worry, I'll tell her. Don't you tell her, Henrietta. Let me."

Henrietta nodded. "Well, you make sure you do

that now, hear? You should have told her before."

"I know."

"She's going to have to think of some good punishment for doing all of that without telling her," Henrietta said.

I shrugged. I didn't want to say "So what?" but that's what I felt. I had given the ball to Davy and Davy loved it. That was all that mattered.

"This isn't my ball, though," Davy said.

"What do you mean?" I asked. "Of course it's your ball. It says right on it 'For Davy.'"

"It's *our* ball," Davy said. "We'll share it. Six months in my house and six months in yours. Like we said. Only I keep it first."

"It's your ball, Davy," I said. "It's your ball all the time. Jackie Robinson meant it for you."

"Well, if he meant it for me, I can do what I want with it, and I want you to keep it for me six months out of the year. And Henrietta, you listen to me. When I die, that ball goes to Sam. You're not to let Elliot have it."

"Oh, go put it in your will, Pops," she said. "Take care of it yourself, when you come home. I don't want no truck with no balls."

"You heard me, Henrietta," Davy said in a stern voice. He was still kind of whispering, but even so he could make his voice stern. There was a twinkle in his eye though, and I knew laughter lay right behind the sternness. "It's a sin to disobey the wishes of the dead," he teased, "and if you do I'll come back to haunt you. Every time the Dodgers lose I'll haunt you."

"If the Dodgers lose it sure won't be my fault," Henrietta said.

"You just see to it that my wishes are followed," Davy said, "and you got nothing to worry about."

The nurse who had been coming down the room bed by bed got to Davy now. She looked at me and then she looked at Henrietta. "Immediate family?" she asked Henrietta, raising her eyebrows.

"You better run along now, Sammy," Henrietta said. "The nurse has got to do all her fussing with Pops and then he'll probably sleep for a while."

Davy had sunk back into his pillows. The little spurt of energy he had exhibited when I had given him the ball seemed to have faded. He shut his eyes for a moment, and then he opened them again and looked at me. "I am sure glad you came, Sammy. I sure am glad you came. Who they playing today?"

He didn't even know. He was really sick. "The Pirates," I said.

"Root hard," he said. "Root hard enough for both of us."

"I will," I promised.

"I'll be home in time for the Series," he said. "You'll come down and listen to it with me on the radio."

"Right," I said. It was about all I could say. I wasn't good at making my voice normal, like Henrietta.

"Go along now," the nurse said.

"Goodbye, Davy."

"Goodbye, Sam." He lifted his hand up off the bed. I took it. He closed his fingers around mine. "See you soon," he whispered. Then he let go and shut his eyes.

"So long," I whispered back, and then I left as quickly as I could.

Elliot was waiting for me in the sunroom at the end of the corridor, where patients who could walk around went to sit. He drove me back to his house, where I got my bike and rode home. I ran up to my room fast as I could, because I didn't want to meet my mother or my sisters or anyone else.

There was no magic in the ball. He loved it, but there was no magic in it. It was not going to cure him, the way deep down in my heart I had somehow thought it would. I knew that. My whole self knew that now.

I threw myself on my bed and cried and cried. I cried and cried as if I would never stop. After a while there was a knock on my door. I didn't answer, but my mother came in anyway. My face was buried in my pillow and she couldn't see it.

"Where have you been?" she asked.

"To see Davy," I answered, my voice muffled by my sobs and the pillow.

She put her hand on my shoulder and gently turned me over, and looked into my face. She touched my forehead with her hand, and then she went to the sink in the corner of the room. With cool water she wet a wash cloth which she put across my face. After a while, I stopped crying and fell asleep.

I guess I cried myself out that Sunday, because a week or so later, when Mother told me that Davy had died, I didn't cry at all. It was no surprise to me.

I was listening to the game in my room when she came up to tell me. She didn't say much, and I didn't say much. After she left, I turned off the radio.

When a Jew dies, they just stick the body in the ground. That's how they did with my father. Before twenty-four hours had passed, they had his body in the ground.

Davy was a Christian and Christians do it differently. At least, Henrietta was a Christian. She belonged to the AME Zion Church. AME, I found out that day, stands for African Methodist Episcopal, and they believe in viewings. As a matter of fact, most Christians do. Viewings, or wakes, or whatever you want to call them.

My mother made me go with her to Davy's. I didn't really want to go, but Mother said Henrietta expected it. It was funny, because she had not let me or Sara go to my father's funeral at all. Sara always held that against Mother. She felt that she had been pushed away from what really was important that day, as if somehow our father's death wasn't supposed to matter to her, or as if Mother didn't want her around. And Mother now knew that Sara was resentful about not seeing our father buried, and I guess she had decided not to make the same mistake twice. Only she was a little mixed up, because I didn't care about having missed our father's funeral, and I didn't care if I missed this one either.

But you find out when you love people that you have to do a lot of things that are expected of you. It's a pain in the neck, and there were times that week when I thought it would be better not loving anyone at all.

The trouble with this viewing thing is that they have the body lying right out there in front of everybody. That doesn't bother most people. It didn't bother my mother. But it bothered me. When we got to the funeral parlor and I saw that casket open in the front of the room, I thought I was going to throw up. I had no intention of going up and looking in it, like everyone else was doing. But here comes that business about what's expected again.

My mother and I went over to Henrietta, who was sitting in the front row. Henrietta stood up to greet us, and my mother put her arms around Henrietta and gave her a big kiss, and she pressed Elliot's hand. Also the hand of Davy's sister from North Carolina, who never did stop crying the whole time. "You know how bad we feel," Mother said to Henrietta. "I don't think I ever knew a man any finer than Davy."

"Thank you, Mrs. Greene," Henrietta said formally. She wasn't crying at all. "He certainly liked working for you better than for anyone else he'd ever worked for. You sure helped make his last couple of years happy ones." She looked at me. I was just sort of standing there, my hands hanging at my sides. "You too, Sammy," she said. "You sure helped make Pops' last years happy ones. Did you look at him, Sammy? He looks so natural, just like he's sleeping. Mr. Skene sure did a marvelous job." Mr. Skene was the man who owned the funeral parlor.

"I don't want to look at him," I said, very quickly.

My mother glared at me. I knew I had committed the supreme error, but I could not help it. My desire not to look at Davy's dead body was stronger than any manners I had ever learned, or any love I had ever felt. It was stronger even than my shyness.

Henrietta took my hand. "You come with me," she said firmly. "He won't frighten you. He looks like he's sleeping."

I went with her. Once again my shyness, my shame, proved to be stronger than I was. It was either go with her or stand there, protesting and pulling, in front of that whole funeral parlor full of black men in their brown and navy suits and black women in their dark starched cotton summer dresses. Elliot and my mother followed.

Well, to make a long story short, I looked. I looked into that great rich brown mahogany box, all lined with creamy satin. In one way Henrietta was right. The body, clothed in a brand-new suit and with its eyes tight shut and its hands folded in an attitude of prayer, did not frighten me.

In another way, though, Henrietta was wrong. That body didn't look like Davy sleeping. It didn't look like Davy at all. That is, it looked like Davy, but it wasn't Davy. It was a wax dummy of Davy, and it bore about the same relationship to him that one of those monster dolls in a store window bears to a living, breathing human being walking around on the street outside the store. There's a kind of resemblance, but you'd never mistake the one for the other.

That's what I said. It just came right out of me. "That isn't Davy," I said.

Henrietta was insulted. "What do you mean?" she said, her annoyance clear in her voice. "Of course that's Davy. Mr. Skene did a wonderful job."

Elliot laughed. Maybe his laugh, sharp and bitter, was the first laugh that had ever been laughed in that room. "Henrietta," he said, "don't you know what that boy is talking about? And you're supposed to be the religious one in the family!"

Henrietta turned her frowning glance on Elliot. "Now, what are *you* talking about?" she asked.

"The real Davy isn't there," Elliot said. "The boy seen that. That's just Davy's shell, there in the box, left behind like an old snakeskin."

I nodded. "That's right, Henrietta," I said. "That's what I meant."

Elliot's voice was suddenly soft, all the sarcasm gone out of it. "And where did the real Davy go, Sammy? You know so much, can you tell me where the real Davy went?"

"I don't know," I replied. "I don't know anything."

"That's a hard question for him to answer," my mother said. "After all, in our religion we don't teach much about heaven and all those things. We don't talk about it much."

"Mostly they're too busy trying to teach us to read Hebrew," I explained. "They don't have time to bother with anything else."

"Well, I can tell you where he went," Henrietta said firmly. "His soul is sitting on the right hand of Jesus this very minute."

There wasn't anything I could say to that, but it gave me lots to think about. A thin, old, yellow lady, as frail and transparent as a pin oak leaf in November, came over to Henrietta then, so my mother and I went to the back of the room and sat down for a while. Then we left.

Outside it was night. Riding home in the car I talked more to my mother than I usually did. Black night all around and being cozy inside a car always made me feel talkative, the way I had felt when I was driving home from ball games with Davy.

I asked my mother: "Do you think Davy's soul is in heaven, with God?"

My mother was always honest. She never said something to be comforting if she didn't think it was the truth. "I don't know," she answered me. "But you were right. That body in the coffin wasn't Davy."

"I don't think it's fair," I said. "I don't think it's fair that both Dad and Davy died."

"Life isn't fair," my mother replied. "No one ever said it would be. But as long as you remember people, they're not really dead. That's what I believe. That's the immortality I believe in."

"I don't remember Dad very well," I muttered.

"But you'll remember Davy. You're old enough to remember Davy all your life."

That was no comfort to me. At that moment I

wished I'd never known Davy at all. If I'd never known him, I wouldn't have had this funny feeling in my stomach right then. I wouldn't have had this big empty hole, this big nothing down there. My skin wouldn't have felt all dried up like an old prune. If I hadn't known him, if I hadn't loved him, Davy could have died and it wouldn't have made any difference to me at all. I would be just the way I had been before I'd known him. I'd be better off than I was, because right then I thought the hole in my stomach was going to last the rest of my life. I thought the emptiness I felt where I was supposed to have a heart was never going to go away.

The next day we had to go to the funeral, and there was a lot of singing and carrying on. It was the sister who carried on, and a few of the women friends, answering the preacher back with moans and groans as he prayed. Henrietta did not carry on. I understood how Henrietta felt. I did not carry on either, but something in me wished that I could. "If I could cry," I thought, "if I could only cry maybe I could fill up this hole in my stomach." But at the same time, I disapproved of the ones who were carrying on. I had the feeling they weren't really grieving for Davy, only pretending to grieve, and I was glad I was a man and not crying.

It was a long trip to the cemetery. They didn't have one for black people in our town. We had to go all the way to Riverton, in the southern part of the state. By the time we got home again, it was dark.

Mother said, "The girls must have eaten by now. I'll get Harry to fix us some supper." Harry was the new cook.

"I'm not hungry," I said. "I'm going to my room."

"What are you going to do up there?" my mother asked.

"I'm going to rest," I answered patiently, as if I were speaking to a child. "I'm tired."

"Rest?" she repeated, kind of stupidly, I thought. "Just rest? Why don't you listen to the ball game?"

"No!" I cried out, very sharply. "I don't want to listen to the ball game."

"But Sammy," she began to protest. "You *can't* just lie there."

"There is no ball game tonight," I improvised quickly.

"*Someone's* playing ball tonight," my mother said. "Somewhere, someone is playing ball."

"No," I said. "There's no ball game on tonight."

"That's a lie, isn't it, Sammy?" she said. "That's a lie."

I shrugged. I had decided not to say anything more. My mother realized that. She went into the kitchen, and I went up to my room.

I took my radio off my night table and put it on my bureau. Then I took off my shoes and lay down on my bed, looking at the ceiling with wide, dry eyes that would not shut. What was the point of listening to the ball game? Who could I talk about it with? Al? Mickey? What did they know? What did they care?

Beside me, on my night table, were my glove and a bald old tennis ball. I picked up the ball and began to toss it at the ceiling. Plop, it landed in my glove. Plop, against the ceiling. Plop, into my glove. Plop, plop, plop, plop. I must have thrown that ball against the ceiling a thousand times until above me there was a whole mess of black marks. It wasn't the first time I'd thrown that ball against the ceiling, not by a mile, but it was the first time I'd thrown it against the ceiling for so long a stretch.

After a while, I guess my mother heard the endless plop, plop, plop, plop. She came into my room without even knocking. "For God's sake, Sammy," she said angrily. "How many times have I told you not to throw that ball against the ceiling? I've told you it's going to leave marks on the white paint . . ." She grabbed the ball out of my glove and looked up. "See?" she said. "What did I tell you? Now I'm going to have to have that ceiling repainted." Then, suddently, her anger seemed to fizzle out. "You must have been doing this for hours," she said, shaking her head, "to make the ceiling black as all that."

She went over to the bureau and got my radio. She put it down next to me on the night table. "Don't feel too sorry for yourself for too long," she said drily. "It doesn't pay. Take it from one who knows." Then she left my room, shutting the door behind her. She took the tennis ball with her.

I had made up my mind that I would not turn on that radio. I was very angry at my mother. Who did she think she was, interfering with my misery? Why hadn't she told me that Davy's soul was in heaven and done me some good? She didn't know for sure, one way or the other. She could have fibbed a little, to make me feel better. And maybe I could have believed her fib, for a little while.

But I knew that I would not have believed her fib, and that made me angrier than ever. I thought of getting up and scrabbling through my closet to see if I could find another tennis ball, but I didn't.

Instead, I stared at the radio, torturing myself, willing myself not to turn it on. In spite of myself, I could not help thinking about the game. It was a very important game. Every game was important so late in the season, with the Dodgers in second place, one and a half games behind the Cardinals. The third-place Phillies were fourteen games out, so the contest was strictly between the Cards and the Dodgers. Some people didn't think it was a contest. Some people thought the Cards had the pennant all tied up. But I knew better. If there was one thing Davy had taught me, it was that the time to really get nervous about the Dodgers was when they were ahead. They were never less out than when they were down.

In spite of telling myself that I didn't want to listen to the game because I had no one to share it with, I really did want to know what was happening, just for my own sake. And yet I felt that to turn that radio on would have been some kind of betrayal of the love, and the anger, and the grief I had been feeling all week—all the emotions which I thought I'd have been better off if I'd never known, and yet which I stubbornly clung to as if I'd cease to exist once they ceased to exist.

"Maybe right at this very second Jackie Robinson is hitting his seventeenth home run of the season," I thought. "Maybe right at this very moment he's stealing the eighty-third base of his three major-league seasons. Maybe Joe Hatten is pitching a no-hitter. Maybe Herman Wehmeier is pitching a no-hitter!" Wehmeier was a Cincinnati pitcher who had beaten Brooklyn the two previous times he'd gone against them. A no-hitter on his part was a possibility—a horrible possibility, but one nevertheless, and one I ought to know about.

Davy ought to know about it too, wherever he was—

just in case he was somewhere. And since we all seemed to agree that he wasn't in that mahogany box in the ground, maybe, just maybe, he *was* somewhere —somewhere else.

So I reached over and flicked on the radio. I did it very quickly, and with the tiniest gesture possible, so that it would seem that the radio had kind of turned itself on, that I had nothing to do with it. I didn't have to tune it in. It was always set at WHN, 1050 on your radio dial.

Red Barber's soft, unattached southern voice flowed around me. "The count is two balls, one strike," he said. Then there was a long pause. "Wehmeier is winding up and he lets go with a high hard one. Strike two. Jackie never even saw it." Another long pause. Then Red Barber began to fill in the time. "Two outs in the top of the seventh. Score tied up at one all. Wehmeier's pitching superb ball tonight. The Dodgers are going to have to go pretty far to pull this one out of the fire."

I leaned into the radio. Things were bad. Two outs and two strikes. Only one strike between the Dodgers and the end of the inning—for them. And just two more at-bats between the Dodgers and the end of the game. I didn't want that game to be over. It was too soon for the game to be over.

"Hit it, Jackie," I said. "Go ahead, Jackie, hit it.

123

Hit it for Davy, Jackie. Hit it for your friend, Davy."

Red Barber was talking again. "Wehmeier leans back—way, way back. But wait—he's stopping. He's straightening up. He puts the ball in his glove, and wipes his hand on his pants. He's looking at his hand —now he's wiping it again. I guess he wants to make sure this ball is a good one."

"Damn that Wehmeier," I said. "He's trying to put Jackie off. All keyed up to swing, and then the damn pitcher doesn't throw. You hit it, Jackie," I repeated. "You hit it. You got to hit it this time." My prayer was a counterpoint against Red Barber's voice.

"Wehmeier seems satisfied, finally. He's winding up again, slowly, slowly—and now he lets go—Jackie swings and hits it. It's a good one, it's a good one!" Red Barber's voice rose high with excitement. "A line drive past Peanuts Lowrey in left field. Peanuts makes the play off the wall and pegs it to Bloodworth at second. But Jackie's going to make it! Jackie's going to stretch it into a double!"

I heard what Red Barber was saying with half an ear. I only knew that Jackie Robinson had saved me once again. In my mind's eye I could see him tearing around the base paths with more speed than any other man in baseball. I could see him cutting first base sharply and heading for second, and in my mind, where nothing ever dies, I can see him still, to this very day, running from base to base in the top of the seventh inning, between the second and third out, in a brand-new baseball game that will never, ever be over.

Also from Beech Tree Books

Baseball Fever
by Johanna Hurwitz

Chancy and the Grand Rascal
by Sid Fleischman

Jayhawker
by Patricia Beatty

Lost on a Mountain in Maine
by Donn Fendler as told to Joseph Egan

Smugglers' Island
by Avi

Soccer Circus
by Jamie Gilson

Trapped in the Slickrock Canyon
by Gloria Skurzynski

Vinegar Pancakes and Vanishing Cream
by Bonnie Pryor